TROUBLE

It was one o'clock in the morning! "Sam, I have to go home, please!" My folks would be furious. I'd told them I was going to a football game and they expected me home by eleven at the latest. Sam heard the urgency in my voice and we left immediately.

On the way home he tried to reassure me. "Relax, JT. We'll tell them we had a flat tire on the way home."

"We nothing. I'm not even supposed to be out with guys unless I ask them. And then, can you imagine them saying, 'Oh, sure. Have a good time with Sam Bensen, the guy who got suspended the first day of school.'"

"Hey, you really are scared, aren't you? Don't worry, most parents just threaten, they don't do anything." Sam kept trying to reassure me.

As I turned to look at him I felt soft, moist lips brushing mine. For a moment they lingered and then they were gone. In that instant I forgot about being late, I forgot about making up lies and even what year it was.

I had never really been in trouble like this before. I wondered what would happen. For some unexplainable reason I suddenly didn't care.

RECKLESS

A TEENAGE LOVE STORY

JEANETTE MINES RYAN

AN AVON  FLARE BOOK

RECKLESS is an original publication of Avon Books. This work has never before appeared in book form.

AVON BOOKS
A division of
The Hearst Corporation
959 Eighth Avenue
New York, New York 10019

Library of Congress Cataloging in Publication Data

Ryan, Jeanette Mines.
  Reckless.

  (An Avon/Flare book)
  Summary: On her first day of high school, Jeannie Tanger meets Sam Bensen, a handsome troublemaker, and decides that she can change him.
  I. Title.
PZ7.R952Re 1983   [Fic]   83-3854
ISBN 0-380-83717-X

First Flare Printing, June, 1983

FLARE BOOKS TRADEMARK REG. U. S. PAT. OFF. AND IN OTHER COUNTRIES, MARCA REGISTRADA, HECHO EN U. S. A.

Printed in the U. S. A.

WFH 10 9 8 7 6 5 4 3 2

To John and Marie for their endurance
I love you both

To Pam for her encouragement
Thank you

Chapter 1

The night before my first day of high school I hardly slept at all. First I was worried that the alarm wouldn't go off. And when I finally fell asleep, I dreamt that I missed the bus and ran to school only to find the doors were locked. After tossing and turning all night, I eventually gave up in frustration and got out of bed just as the alarm went off.

I had already picked out the clothes I was going to wear, but this morning they looked all wrong. Trying to find the perfect outfit, I tried on four pairs of jeans, six blouses, and at least three sweaters. In the end I wore the exact jeans, blouse, and vest I had started with. For forty-five minutes I struggled to get my hair perfect. But I was convinced it looked like a comb had never touched it. Then I knew I couldn't postpone leaving for school any longer or I'd be late.

All the way there I was scared to death. Every gruesome story I'd ever heard about high school raced through my mind. I desperately wanted to do well. I vowed right then and there to make a good first impression on both the kids and the teachers.

When I got to school I found my first-hour science class. Sliding into a seat near the window I looked around for someone I knew. No such luck. Then I panicked. Was I in the right room? Was I even in the right class? Afraid to display my complete stupidity as a freshman, I didn't ask anyone.

I was so busy studying the back of my science book it took me a second to realize someone was speaking to me.

"Hey, this teacher is so bad. I sure wish I hadn't got stuck with him again."

I looked directly into the brownest eyes I had ever seen. "Oh, really," I managed to mumble.

"Yeah, I had Jakness last year and he failed me. I got a B on the final, but he said it was necessary to do more than pass the test in order to pass the class. Like maybe I could come to more than five classes a semester. So here I am again in this boring, useless class."

"That's, that's too bad," I stammered. Would my great command of the English language ever return so I could speak like an intelligent human being? But he didn't seem to notice and kept right on talking.

"In case you don't know me, I'm Sam Bensen, and you?"

"Jeannie, Jeannie Tanger."

By this time the room had filled and the famed Mr. Jakness strolled in and wrote "Science 101" on the board, so at least I knew I was in the right place. When the bell rang, Jakness began the usual first-day-of-the-semester lecture. While he talked, I secretly scrutinized Sam as he lounged at his desk with his feet propped on the seat in front of him.

Around those gorgeous brown eyes I saw a dark smooth face with a huge head of brown curly hair. He had on a pair of very tight and revealing blue jeans, Nike running shoes, and a T-shirt that proclaimed "I do it right." I briefly wondered if he did do it right, or if he did it at all.

Mr. Jakness took roll and when he got to Sam's name said, "Mr. Bensen, nice to see you, hope to continue seeing you this semester."

Sam just smiled, and when Mr. Jakness called the next name Sam glanced over and winked at me—or so I thought. Finally the bell rang and as Sam hurried out the door he whispered, "See you around, JT."

It took me a couple of seconds to realize he was talking to me—no one had ever called me JT before.

The rest of the day passed quickly. I managed to find all my classes and never got suckered into buying an elevator pass for a nonexistent elevator from a hotshot sophomore.

After school I met Renee, my best friend from grammar school, by my locker. She was in her usual vivacious mood. "Isn't this place something? I just knew I'd love it. There are so many cute guys I can hardly control myself. I met this guy—his name is Brian and he's on the football team—I'm in love! Now I have to find out where his locker is." Her short blond hair bounced as she glanced in every direction. Since she was only five foot two she had to stand on her tiptoes to see around everyone in the hall.

Renee and I had known each other since first grade. We spent a lot of time together and she did most of the talking. But if something was bothering me she always could tell, and was the only person I knew who could get me to say what was really on my mind.

In fact, I guess Renee was about the only close friend I had. I had a lot of acquaintances, but not the kind whom I'd talk to about my parents' fighting, or my dream to work in Washington, D. C., someday, or the fact that I was terrified of heights. She was the only one who knew how scared I'd been this morning. Renee had been a little nervous too, but she viewed high school as the ultimate challenge of her life and from the talking she was doing, I was convinced she wouldn't have any problem becoming a success quickly.

Renee chattered all the way to the bus stop and home. We exchanged tidbits about our classes, our teachers, and our crummy schedules. Once I started to tell her about Sam, but then I stopped. I really didn't know what to say. I was afraid somehow Sam's tight jeans compared to Brian's football career just wouldn't make it with Renee so I kept quiet. I wondered if Renee even noticed if Brian's pants were tight.

When I got home, I retrieved the evening newspaper from the bushes and went in the house to relax. Since it was my brother Tom's turn to get supper, I got comfortable in the living room. The headlines were the usual, but I read them all anyway. I have this thing about always reading the paper from the front to the back. Besides, I like to read anything I can about Washington, D. C. Ever since I saw a movie in fifth grade about the President and all the people who work for him, I've known that's where I want to be and I'll never get there by watching soap operas. Not that I don't like soap operas, but it's not one of the things I often admit to Renee.

I read as fast as I could because I knew when Dad got home it would be good-bye newspaper. Why Dad always figured he was entitled to the paper first was beyond me. We all worked hard. But I did hope Dad would be in a better mood today than he had been lately.

"Hi, kids." Dad threw a blue sweatshirt and his favorite baseball hat toward the rack on his way to the living room. "I hope supper is about ready. Hey, Jeannie, can I have the paper? I'm dying to see what they said about the game last night."

And I'm dying to see what great advice Ann Landers is dishing out today, but I guess I won't find out now. "Sure, Dad. How was work?"

"Same old stuff. I wish they'd decide if they are going to go out on strike or not. This waiting is driving me crazy. Did your mother call? I wish she'd be here when I get home." Dad's nearly bald head was glistening with sweat. After working in the factory all day, he came home hot, sweaty, and tired. He dropped his large frame into his easy chair.

"Yeah, she said she'd be late, Dad," Tom bellowed from the kitchen.

"Oh, not again." Dad sighed as he turned to the

sports page. Mom is a secretary for a lawyer downtown and lately she's been putting in a lot of overtime. Dad gets annoyed, but doesn't say too much because he knows how much we need the money, especially if he goes out on strike.

I went to the kitchen to see if Tom needed any help. Renee would laugh if she were here. She can't believe Tom and I take turns getting supper. But my folks believe in everybody pitching in so both of us learned pretty early how to cook, vacuum, take out the garbage, mow the grass, and everything else around the house.

As usual, Tom had everything under control. Tom is my seventeen-year-old wonder brother — 6'1", blond, blue eyed, intelligent, considerate, athletic, and downright disgusting sometimes. Trying to follow his act has always been a real problem for me. Not that I'm ugly or anything, or stupid either. I'm what people call cute. Actually, I'm pretty smart too, but I try real hard not to let anybody know I'm Tom's sister, especially teachers who know Tom. If there's one thing I can't stand it's when a teacher starts doing a number on how good my brother did and how they hope I'm just like him.

"How was your first day at Lincoln?" Tom asked.

"O.K., I managed to find my way around," I replied.

"How do your classes look?"

"Not bad. I have Jakness for science. Did you have him?"

"Yeah, I did and he's quite a character."

"Oh, yeah, like how?" I figured I might as well get as much info as I could.

"Well, for one thing, he has this fancy red Corvette and when he first came to Lincoln he was always challenging kids to race him, but I don't think he does that anymore."

"No kidding. Isn't that a little weird for a teacher?"

"Yeah, but Jakness isn't your normal teacher. In

fact, I don't think Jakness is normal at all. He's always trying to be a comedian, too, so be sure and laugh at his sick jokes."

"He didn't seem too funny today." Of course I wasn't even sure if he'd made any funny jokes or not. All I had concentrated on was that beautiful body sitting next to me.

"Another thing, Jeannie, if you want to stay on his good side be sure to come to class. He has a thing about kids cutting."

I don't usually mention my friends to Tom, but I found myself saying, "Yeah, a guy sitting next to me said this is his second time around. Hey, maybe you know him—Sam Bensen?"

Tom's smile became a frown. "Yeah, I know him, and you'll be smart not to know him, Jeannie. He's trouble, real trouble."

"What do you mean?" My heart was pounding. Here my brother was insulting my new love with strange insinuations.

"Never mind. Just take my advice and stay away from him, and don't ever get in a car with him." The creases around Tom's eyes and the tone of his voice told me to drop the subject, so I did.

Mom finally arrived home at seven o'clock and I was famished. Our family has this weird notion that we should all eat together and everyone gets a chance to tell what they did that day. Sort of a strange custom, or so Renee says, but I actually kind of like it. That is if Dad doesn't take over.

As soon as we sat down, Mom asked, "Jeannie, did everything go all right your first day?"

"Yeah, Mom, no problems," I responded.

"Did you find all your classes and get all your books?"

"Sure, you'd have thought I was a sophomore the way I sauntered around the halls," I bragged. Actually, I didn't want Mom to worry. Sometimes she just doesn't realize I'm fourteen and can fend for myself these days.

"Margaret, the factory was in an uproar again today," Dad chimed in.

"Really, Al?" Mom turned to Dad, smiled, and then looked back at me. "Did you meet any new kids, Jeannie?" Mom was more interested in my day than Dad's, and I really wanted to tell her about it. But as usual Dad kept butting in so Mom finally listened to him relate the events of his boring day.

After I did the dishes, I excused myself and went to my room, hoping Mom would come up so we could talk.

Mom never came up though. I heard her and Dad arguing in the living room after Tom had gone to his room. Lately it seemed that Dad was on Mom's back about everything. Ever since she started working overtime Dad had been angry. I didn't remember them arguing like this before.

Mom is small, slim, and very pretty. Her short brown hair curves softly around her face and you can't help but notice her startling blue eyes. I suppose Dad worries about her around all those successful professional men. He tries to act liberated, but I think deep down he thinks Mom's place is in the home. I'm not happy about Mom being gone all the time either, but she likes her job and Dad likes the money so he shouldn't give her a hard time. Finally I gave up trying to figure it all out and let my dreams of gorgeous Sam put me to sleep.

Chapter 2

I could hardly wait to get to science class the next morning. Renee chattered all the way down the corridor, but I couldn't concentrate on her words at all. I mumbled "Oh, yeah" a lot.

Sam wasn't there. I couldn't believe he had nerve enough to cut classes the second day of school. Why was I so disappointed because a guy I hardly knew wasn't in class? Disappointed, nothing—I was miserable! I'm sure Mr. Jakness lectured for an hour, but what he said I'll never know.

By lunchtime, Renee had collected all the school gossip. She filled me in on every upcoming social event, did a monologue on all her teachers, and announced she was positively in love with Brian. He was not only a sophomore football player, but he was a class officer too. Renee was ecstatic. In the last two days she'd met lots of kids, liked her classes, and was absolutely convinced that Lincoln High was the greatest thing that had ever happened to her.

Boy, were we different. I had hardly met anybody and my classes were a drag. Sometimes I wondered how Renee and I were such good friends. Here it was the second day of school and the only thing that had made any impression on me at all in this school of 1,800 kids was a guy named Sam Bensen.

While I thought about Sam, Renee kept talking about her new love. She said Brian knew everything that went on in the school. This morning at his locker he was talking about the kid who already got suspended. "Can you imagine getting suspended the first day of school for almost hitting a teacher? Boy, that Sam Bensen must really be a crazy guy!"

"Sam Bensen?" I practically shouted.

"Yeah, why? Do you know him, Jeannie?" Renee turned to me.

"Well, yes, I mean no. Well, what I mean is, he's in one of my classes and I heard one of the teachers call him by name." Why was I lying to Renee, who was supposed to be my best friend? "Hey, does suspension mean he'll be out for a day or what?"

"He'll be back in three days," a voice behind me announced.

"Hi, Brian," Renee cooed. "I was just talking about you. Meet my friend, Jeannie Tanger."

"Hello." I turned to inspect Renee's new heart-throb. I could see why Renee had fallen so quickly for this tall, good-looking football player. He obviously lifted weights every day and sat under a sunlamp to keep that perfect tan. His very neatly styled black hair just touched his ears. Definitely the all-American boy. But definitely not as good-looking as Sam.

"Hi, Jeannie. Why are you interested in Bensen? He's one guy you'd be smart to avoid. You know, he almost decked Wilson, his math teacher. How stupid can a guy be on the first day of school? Besides, he doesn't have the time to fool around. He's on probation from last year. He was expelled for drugs or something."

"No kidding!" Renee was fascinated. "What happened?"

My mouth was dry and my stomach felt sick.

Brian continued, "Rumor had it that he was selling drugs in the bathroom. When the truant officer and Wilson opened the door, he dropped a match in the wastebasket and started a fire so he'd have time to stash the stuff."

Renee was curious and I was dying. She asked, "Did they ever find the stuff he hid?"

"No, they were too busy setting off the fire alarm and clearing all of the kids out of the school. We stood outside for half an hour while the firemen paraded around the building in their hip boots. What a joke!"

I barely managed a smile as Brian proceeded to tell us how wonderful he was going to be in the football game on Friday. I was so relieved when the bell rang and I had an excuse to leave for class.

I kept thinking about what Brian had said and what Tom had insinuated. Both guys had given me plenty of warning. Perhaps I should have listened to them, but I didn't. Instead, I found myself even more curious about this brown-eyed handsome guy I had encountered once in my short, boring life.

Friday Renee was so excited about seeing Brian play football that I couldn't refuse her when she begged me to go to the game with her. It's not that I'm opposed to sports, it's just that I'd rather be a part of something than sit on the sidelines and watch. Tom and I played a lot when I was a kid, so I could handle a basketball pretty well and I was respectable enough when it came to hitting a softball or kicking a football. Watching the sport just wasn't in me. I should have known, though, that Renee was more interested in boy-watching than in football-watching.

Even though it was a beautiful September evening and the Lincoln High cheerleaders were out in full force, I was bored to death. Maybe because the band was doing a good job of being out of rhythm with the drumbeat and Lincoln was losing fourteen to zero.

"Hi, JT," a deep voice from behind surprised me. "I see you must really be enjoying the game, since you haven't smiled or clapped once in the last ten minutes." Then he laughed.

I turned and there he was! The person who had occupied my entire mind for at least ninety-five percent of the time in the last week. "Sam! I thought you were suspended."

"Hey, from school, sweetheart, not from the social events of Lincoln High."

Sweetheart! No one had ever called me sweetheart before. My side was hurting too. Finally I realized Renee was going to crack one of my ribs soon if I didn't acknowledge her.

"Oh, Sam, this is Renee."

"Hi." Sam looked Renee up and down and then smiled.

"Renee, Sam Bensen." God, he's gorgeous, I thought again.

"Hello," Renee stammered. She was quickly turning red, since she didn't know how to respond to his bold stare. I could see her doing a fast scrutiny of Sam. His mop of curly hair wasn't combed and he had on an old jean jacket that looked like it had seen its best days about five years ago. His shirt was open not only at the collar, but halfway down his chest. I just knew what conclusion Renee would come to about anybody who so blatantly flaunted his body. His jeans were faded, but clean, and I couldn't help but notice again how well they fit in all the right places. I saw, or rather felt, Renee's decision about Sam. Her brow was furrowed, but she continued, "So you're Sam Bensen. You have quite a reputation around here. Are any of the rumors we hear true?"

Sam smiled at Renee for at least thirty seconds before he answered. He must have sensed her nervousness. He stretched his legs out in front of him and put his elbows on the bleacher seat behind and relaxed all five foot eight inches of his frame. "Renee, darling, what you've heard is probably only part of my lewd and sordid past. Would you like to hear about the time I kept one of the cheerleaders out all night?" He laughed again.

"I don't think so. If you'll excuse me, I see one of

my friends calling me." Renee gave me a look of total shock and vanished.

Sam couldn't stop laughing. "Is that really one of your friends?"

"Yeah, a good friend, too."

"No kidding? That's hard to believe. She doesn't seem your type and definitely not mine. You, you're another story, JT. The reserved and intelligent type appeals to me. Especially those that have long, brown hair that shines when they turn their head. I also go for bodies that are curved in the right places, if you know what I mean, JT?"

I couldn't respond. I should have said something to defend Renee, but instead I laughed, thinking how carefully I had analyzed Sam's body and all the time he'd been doing the same thing to me.

"You know what I mean, JT?" Sam repeated his remark just to make sure I'd caught his meaning. I decided the best response to him was no response at all, so I changed the subject.

"JT, what is this JT business? My name is Jeannie."

"Yeah, but to me you're a JT. Jeannie Tanger as well as 'Just Terrific' so, JT." Sam made sure he emphasized what was to be my new name. "Sit back, relax, and enjoy it. I think you and I are headed for great things."

What could I possibly say to him? Somehow those deep brown eyes, that lazy smile and small dimple in his chin were too much for my heart to take and I did just what he suggested. I sat back, relaxed, and for the first time all evening enjoyed myself.

About halfway through the third quarter a guy with long, blond hair approached Sam and whispered to him. I couldn't hear what he said, but Sam got a sly grin on his face. As soon as the fellow left, Sam grabbed my hand and announced we were off to see a more exciting game. I had exactly zero idea what he was talking about and my better judgment told me to wait for Renee. But my better judgment lost out to my sense of adventure and the strange feeling in my head that promised new things if I stuck with Sam. So I gave no resistance as Sam guided me to the parking lot. Somewhere in the back of my head I could hear my brother's voice warning me not to ride with Sam, but I did my best to quiet that nagging thought.

Sam started to get into the driver's seat of an old, beat-up green Volkswagen. "Hey, how can you drive? You're only a sophomore?"

"Get in," he said, motioning toward the door.

Reluctantly I got in and we started out the parking lot. "Are you really sixteen?" I asked Sam.

"Yeah," Sam said, laughing.

"Are you absolutely positive?" He had a twinkle in his eyes and I wasn't quite sure if I should believe him. I had visions of getting picked up for cruising in a stolen car being driven by an unlicensed driver.

"JT, relax, I'm sixteen and this is my car. You see, I had this very old, senile second-grade teacher who refused to pass me on to the wonders of the third grade. I'm sure she lived to regret it because all during my second try in her room snakes appeared in her desk, books disappeared mysteriously, and apples with worms were common presents for her. Strangely enough, I was promoted to third grade even though I had unsatisfactory grades my entire repeated year."

Sam had such a way of telling a story that I couldn't help laughing at the idea of his planting snakes in the poor teacher's desk.

"Where are we going?" I asked when I saw him turn in to a residential neighborhood.

"Well, sweetheart, to a place where the game consists of singing and playing all day long—sometimes all night long, too."

Chapter 3

We drove in silence for a while. I kept thinking of all the rumors I'd heard about Sam. I couldn't believe they were true. I wanted to know as much as I could about this intriguing guy I was with. "Sam," I began, "did you almost hit your math teacher?"

Sam gave me a long look and then answered, "JT, believe none of what you hear and all of what I tell you. Do I really strike you as the type of gentleman that would threaten the life of one of our most distinguished teachers? A man who has dedicated himself to helping the cause of youth. A man who can be trusted, admired, and loved by only those students who are willing to bow down and kiss his sacred algebra book? A man who encourages open discussion as long as he is the only one talking? A man who accuses without knowing the facts? A man who should run for public office because he is dishonest, bigoted, unfair, and stupid? He'd probably win an election with all those qualities going for him."

Sam became more and more angry as his tirade continued. A flicker of hate flashed in his eyes and then was gone as fast as it came. Maybe I was imagining it. Almost instantly he was smiling and grabbing me around the neck and trying to drive all at the same time. I noticed he never did answer the question I'd asked. I wondered why he was so mad at Wilson, his math teacher.

Just then we arrived at the so-called game and the playing field turned out to be a big old frame house in a rather quiet part of town. The house belonged to Jeb, the kid with the long blond hair from the football game. "Jeb's parents drink a lot and are hardly ever home, so Jeb does just about what he wants to when he wants to." Sam filled me in on these details as we walked up the front steps.

The house was a wreck. Beer cans were everywhere; one was propping open the oven door. Newspapers were strewn all over the furniture. Amid the rubble Jeb was busy rolling a joint and some of the kids looked like it wasn't the first one of the evening. That relaxed, who-cares, don't-bother-me-look was on the faces of a few kids sitting on the living room floor. Now, don't get the idea that I'm big on drugs or anything, but in our school there were a few older guys who used to make sure there was a steady supply available for anyone who could afford the price. A guy from our eighth-grade class was high most of the time, so I knew the look well.

Jeb grinned. "Want a joint, Sam?"

"No thanks, Jeb," Sam replied.

"How about you, JT?"

"No, not right now," I said. "JT, why did he call me JT, Sam?" I whispered.

"Because that's your name, isn't it, sweetheart?" There suddenly appeared that sly, yet knowing smile on Sam's lips. Had Sam been talking about me to Jeb, I wondered?

"Yeah, I guess so." From that moment on I accepted the fact that I was JT. I liked it. The name was all mine, even if I hadn't thought of it.

Everybody seemed to know Sam. He called them all by name and introduced me around. They all smiled and seemed friendly enough. I hadn't remembered seeing any of them at school, but then I had only been looking for Sam all week and hadn't really gotten to know many new kids. I made a mental note to try harder in school next week to make some new friends.

Sam interrupted my thoughts. "JT, go ahead and have some grass if you want; it just isn't my style. I go for beer when I need a good high."

"Thanks, but no. I'm not really into smoking, either."

"Great, let's go to the kitchen and see what we can find."

I followed Sam to the refrigerator.

"Here, have a beer." Sam pressed one in my hand. I didn't have nerve enough to tell him I didn't drink, either. I took a swallow and it almost made me gag.

"I see you're an experienced beer drinker," quipped Sam as he took a long, slow swallow. "Hang in there, kid, you'll get used to it."

"Yeah," I lamely responded. The second taste didn't improve so I simply held the beer. I figured I could practice the art of deception as well as the next person.

Sam had a quick three beers and his mood changed from funny to funnier. He told story after story about his infamous school career. The party moved into the kitchen as Sam got wound up.

"When I was in third grade, I found an old pocket-knife in the alley one day. I decided to test the cutting quality of this newfound treasure on the top of our school desks. So, during reading when the teacher was occupied with the Sparrows or Bluejays or Twee-tie Brains, as I liked to call them, I carved the name of the teacher's favorite student in the desk top. After lunch our teacher was going crazy!

"She wanted to know who had done such malicious damage to a sacred piece of government property. None of us even knew what she was talking about. Us third-graders weren't into words of more than two syllables. And there was poor Mary, the teacher's pet, crying her eyes out. Her nice, clean desk was all ruined and she wasted no time in pointing me out as the culprit. Of course, I denied it with my most innocent smile. But somehow I wasn't believed and I don't know why, do you?" Sam looked at Jeb and Jeb shook his head. "Anyway I spent the next

23

two weeks after school sanding every desk in the third grade, every lousy desk!"

Sam kept us all laughing as he continued telling stories. After his school stories he started to tell about his infamous notoriety with the local police department. It seemed he and Jeb had been in more than one scrap with our city's finest.

"Hey, Jeb, do you remember the time we went for that joyride in the Cadillac?" Sam was laughing and hitting Jeb on the shoulder.

"Yeah," Jeb added, "the police didn't know if they should charge you with theft, driving without a license, or being truant from the fifth grade!"

"Fifth grade?" a kid named Tim asked. "Do you mean to tell us you stole a car, and a Cadillac at that, and went joyriding at the age of ten?"

Sam got a very serious look on his face. "No, I was eleven. I was held back in second grade, as they chose to say in those days. Flunking was out." Now Sam was smiling again and Tim was chuckling.

"I have a feeling you've had more than that one encounter with the police." Tim grinned. "What'd they ever do anyway about that?"

"Well, in the end, the guy who owned the car dropped the charges, because he had left the keys in the car and I think his insurance company wasn't too happy with him. I think my dad went down and begged for forgiveness from the cops on the theory that boys will be boys and I guess it worked. I was turned over to the custody of my parents." Sam finished another beer and threw the can at the garbage in the corner.

Something about Sam's stories bothered me, but I didn't know exactly what—they were sad, yet funny. But I did know they made Sam even more intriguing to me. For a change it was exciting to be with a person like Sam rather than just hearing about him.

Jeb definitely liked the stories. "Hey, tell us about the first time you played daredevil chicken!"

24

For a second I was puzzled and then I remembered that was the game played with real cars. The cars started at a distance apart and then came straight at each other as fast as they could. The first car to veer out of the path of the oncoming car was the loser. I remember reading about it in the paper awhile back. I recalled that one of the kids playing had gotten hurt real bad when his car hit a telephone pole. They had pictures of the car that had been cut right down the middle. I guess they thought realistic photography might discourage kids from the game. But from the way Sam and Jeb were talking it was obviously still popular. Sam was well into his story when I pulled my mind back to the conversation.

"It was down the usual street, Fillmore. I had borrowed a friend's car to go get my dad from work because his car was in the shop. Anyway, I stopped at Arly's and some kid from out of town was bragging about how good he was at chicken. Nobody was taking him on, and I couldn't figure out why. Well, I found out later, but meanwhile I gallantly challenged him and he accepted. Unfortunately, I had never played before and I wasn't sure of the rules. I did know enough not to give up the road and this out-of-town sucker finally had to turn out. But he turned too sharp and smashed some garbage cans at a church. Now you'd think that since he lost and caused all the damage he'd take the blame. But, oh, nooo. It was when the police came to my house later that night that I found out who this out-of-town visitor was."

Sam paused while everyone waited. "Would you believe he was the nephew of the chief of police?" Everyone started laughing. "Now, I'll leave it to your imagination to figure out who the chief of police believed started the game and who in the end was responsible. All my yelling and screaming only got me in lots of trouble with the cops and they never seem to forget me when there's some action."

"I'll bet you didn't play chicken again," Tim said.

"I guess I should have learned my lesson," Sam said, "but I loved that thrill of racing down the street straight at another car. I loved it so much that daredevil chicken has become my favorite sport."

"That's right. And Sam hasn't lost a game yet, or gotten caught by the police again, either," Jeb said, obviously proud of his friend's ability at a game that seemed very deadly to me.

When he finished his story, I glanced at my watch. I couldn't believe it! It was one o'clock in the morning! "Sam, I have to go home, please!" My folks would be furious. I'd told them I was going to a football game and they expected me home by eleven at the latest. Sam heard the urgency in my voice and we left immediately.

On the way home he tried to reassure me. "Relax, JT. We'll tell them we had a flat tire on the way home."

"'We' nothing. I'm not even supposed to be out with guys unless I ask them. And then, can you imagine them saying, 'Oh, sure. Have a good time drinking beer with Sam Bensen, the guy who got suspended the first day of school.'"

"You'll be home before you know it," Sam said, ignoring my sarcastic tone of voice.

"Yeah, I noticed." We were speeding down the side streets at an easy sixty miles an hour. "Aren't you worried about the cops picking you up for speeding?" I was getting more and more nervous. "Especially with beer on your breath?"

"Sweetheart, you have much to learn. Cops appreciate beer drinkers and beautiful young women. So if I'm stopped, I'll offer you as a sacrifice."

Sometimes I just couldn't answer him. I spent the rest of the way home devising a good lie to tell. Dad had a real temper and I didn't want to get him all riled up. When we got about a block away, I said, "Hey, let me out here and I'll walk. Maybe the fresh air will clear my head and get this awful smoke smell off my clothes. Besides, it will give me a little more time to think of some lie that will convince my parents that I have a good reason for getting home at one thirty in the morning."

"Hey, you really are scared, aren't you? Don't worry, most parents just threaten, they don't do anything." Sam kept trying to reassure me.

"Not my parents, they're very quick on the grounding trigger."

"No problem. I'll buy you a fire escape ladder and you can leave any time you want."

"Sam, you're crazy, you know that? I couldn't sneak out of the house."

"JT, you can do anything you want. Stick with me and we'll go far—if you know what I mean."

As I turned to look at him, Sam's face was two inches from mine. I was looking directly into those brown eye wells. I opened my mouth to say good night and I felt soft, moist lips brushing mine. For a moment they lingered and then they were gone. In that instant I forgot about being late, I forgot about making up lies and even what year it was. All I could feel was my heart pounding through my sweater and my whole body felt weak. I had a fleeting glimpse of what all the big deal was about sex. Suddenly I wanted more than a glimpse.

"You better get going" echoed somewhere in the night. Then I realized it was Sam. "See you tomorrow with the ladder."

"Bye." I found myself standing on the sidewalk and I saw red taillights zooming away.

Slowly I started toward the house. I had never been in real trouble like this before. I wondered what would happen. For some unexplainable reason I suddenly didn't care. Sam's brown eyes and provocative blue jeans were all I could see.

"Jeannie, are you all right?" were the first words out of my mother's mouth. "We've been so worried

27

about you. Was there an accident? Did something happen? Where were you?" My mother came hurrying toward me as I opened the door. Her soft brown hair was in disarray, her forehead crinkled in a worried frown that made me feel guilty.

"Mom, relax, I'm fine, everything is O.K. I was with a friend of mine and I just forgot what time it was. I'm sorry, I didn't mean to make you worry." I shut the door behind me.

"Worry? What the hell do you think we've been doing?" My father's voice boomed from the kitchen as he came charging into the front hall. He was still dressed in his work clothes and they looked like they'd been slept in. "You were with a friend? Who gave you permission to go out with a friend till one thirty in the morning? Who do you think you are? You're grounded for a month, you little sneak."

Just then I felt a sharp sting in my cheek and my ear began to ring. I fell back against the closet door. I could hear my mother yelling at my father.

"Al, why in God's name did you do that? She told us where she was and said she was sorry. Have you no recollection of what it was like to be fourteen?" My mother's short frame was dwarfed by my father's tall body.

"No, damn it, and if she ever does it again that slap will only be the beginning. And if you know what's good for you, you'll stop sticking up for her." My father was staring down at my mother; his face was very red.

"Just what is that supposed to mean?" My mother's quiet voice startled me. My father didn't answer. He just looked at both of us, then turned and stormed up the stairs, slamming the bedroom door behind him.

"Jeannie, I'm sorry, I don't know what got into him. Lately he's been acting strangely." My mother turned to me and tried to put her arm around me.

"Stop making excuses for him! You're always sticking up for him!" All my frustration came out against my mother. I wanted to stop, but my mouth seemed out of control. I heard my own voice through a ringing in my ears. "He'll never do that to me again! And I'll never tell him anything again! This house is a prison, I hate it here! At least Sam understands me." I shook her arm away.

"Sam, who is Sam?" My mother felt the rejection, but didn't give up.

"He's the friend I was with tonight. His name is Sam, Sam Bensen." Just saying his name made me feel better.

"Not Sam Bensen?" Tom had heard the commotion and was coming down the stairs. "Jeannie, I told you that guy was trouble and I was right. Look at all the trouble he's caused around here already tonight."

"He hasn't caused any trouble. The trouble is with this family; everybody is always snooping in everyone else's business. If everyone would just leave me alone I'd be fine."

"Jeannie, you know we're just trying to help you and that we love you." Mom tried to calm me down.

"Then just leave me alone, leave me alone, please!" I followed my father's example, racing upstairs and locking my bedroom door.

That good feeling I'd had was completely gone; even thinking of Sam couldn't calm me down. I paced around my bed. My head was a mess, not just where Dad had hit me, but inside where it counted.

I was furious with my dad for striking me, and I was disappointed my mother had defended him—or had she? I really couldn't remember. My brother's remarks annoyed me beyond sensible reasoning and Sam just totally frustrated me. Was this what high school and growing up was all about? I wasn't sure I could take much more. I did know one thing though:

29

never again would I tell my father the truth, and the next time I'd think of a *great* lie. I didn't want to disappoint him. If he thought I was sneaky and dishonest, then I would be just that.

Chapter 4

Saturday dawned into a bright, beautiful fall morning. But I was too depressed to care. At least if it had been raining or even cloudy, I could have had an excuse for being so down.

When I heard Dad leave the house, I ventured downstairs. Tom was fixing breakfast for himself and Mom was in the basement washing clothes. When she came upstairs she didn't look at me, but I could see her eyes were red and swollen. She had tried the old makeup and powder trick, but it hadn't worked very well.

"Jeannie, there's bacon in the refrigerator, if you want some," Mom mumbled.

"Thanks, but cereal's fine, Mom," I softly answered. I knew I had been the cause of her bad night. I wanted to tell her how sorry I was. I wanted her to hug me. I wanted us to declare we still loved each other. But instead, I ate dry Cheerios, looked at the same page of the newspaper without seeing one word, and felt miserable. Tom, for once, had the good sense to be quiet. He did manage to give me a quick wink as he left the kitchen, so at least I knew he didn't hate me.

I was doing the usual Saturday morning duties when the phone rang. I wasn't in any mood to talk, but after three rings it was obvious Mom wasn't going to answer it, so I picked up the receiver.

"Jeannie, it's Renee. Hey, what happened to you last night?" Renee asked. "You just disappeared."

"I left with Sam." The minute I said it, I regretted it.

"Sam! You left with that guy, how could you?"

"What do you mean 'how could I?' You don't even know him."

"I know enough to know he isn't the right kind of guy for you, Jeannie."

"How do you know what kind of guy is right for me?" I snapped.

"Hey, take it easy, Jeannie. I'm your friend, remember?"

"Then don't criticize Sam. I like him. He's nice. He makes me feel good."

"Yeah, I'll bet he feels good. I've heard he does a lot of feeling wherever, whenever he can."

"Oh, Renee, do you believe everything you hear? You don't even know Sam." First Sam criticized Renee. Now Renee was on Sam's case. What was happening? Why couldn't they like each other? I liked both of them.

"Jeannie, forget Sam—he'll just be trouble for you. Besides, Brian's got a date for you tonight. We'll double and go to the movies. You'll have a great time. What do you say?"

Renee was trying so hard. But she just didn't understand. Nobody was like Sam. Nobody.

"Thanks, Renee, but no. Besides, I couldn't if I wanted to. I'm grounded."

"Grounded! Why?"

"Well, I got in late last night and Dad was really mad."

"Where did you go with Sam anyway, Jeannie?" Renee's questioning tone of voice bothered me. How could I tell her about Jeb's house and the beer and pot? She'd never understand.

"Just around. Well, I have work to do. Have a good time tonight, I'll talk to you tomorrow. Bye."

Before Renee could say anything else I hung up. I knew I would regret it later because Renee wouldn't stand for a brush-off like that. But I just wasn't in the mood to discuss my predicament with someone who didn't even know Sam.

The phone rang again. I slowly picked it up. This phone was getting to be more than my nerves could stand.

"Hi, sweetheart, I got the ladder. Where shall I meet you so you can pick it up?" I could hear the laughter in his voice.

"Sam, you don't really have a ladder, do you?" I was incredulous. I glanced in the kitchen to see if Mom could hear who I was talking to.

"Sure. It's one of those fire escape rope ladders. It'll be a cinch for you to sneak it into the house today and then tonight you'll be all set."

"Sam, I'm grounded. I feel terrible and you're making crazy jokes."

"What crazy jokes? I figured you might be grounded so I bought this ladder today at the hardware store and tonight you can use it to sneak out. I have great plans for us. This ladder will help you down and I'll help you up." Sam just laughed.

"You're really serious, aren't you?"

"Of course. Listen, I'll meet you in half an hour at the drugstore on the corner of Archer and Cuyler. You can think of some excuse to go to the drugstore, can't you?"

"I suppose." Was I really agreeing to meet this obviously crazy person?

"Good. See you in half an hour." Sam hung up and I walked slowly to my room.

I couldn't believe myself. Here I was grounded. My head was a mess inside and I was considering meeting Sam to get a rope ladder to sneak out of my room. Life had been so much simpler a week ago.

I went to find Mom. She hadn't been around all morning. In one way that was a relief because I hated to see her feeling so down. It was Dad's fault. Times like this made me almost hate him. He was such a creep sometimes. All he ever thought about was his stupid union and what sport was on the boob tube. I knew he was working overtime this morning but he'd be home by one to see some boring college football game. I decided to take off now so I would be absolutely sure of missing him.

I finally found Mom changing the bedding in her room. "Mom, is it O.K. if I go down to the drugstore? I have to get a couple of things for school." Even though I was grounded I figured Mom would let me out if it wasn't for pleasure.

"Sure, Jeannie, just don't be too long." She still avoided looking at me, but the sadness in her voice was very apparent. I really did love my mother, but I was too afraid to say anything. Sometimes the adult world was so hard to penetrate. So, instead, I just said, "I won't be long. Thanks, Mom." I hurried out the door and straight for the drugstore. The crisp air was a welcome relief after the closeness of our house.

Sam was waiting in his green bug. He was in a no-parking zone, but that obviously didn't concern him.

"Sam, you're in a no-parking zone," I said as I slid in next to him.

"JT, you must stop worrying so much. I won't get a ticket."

"Why are you so sure?" I demanded.

"Because I paid off the local cop last week like always." His face was very serious.

"No, you didn't, you're crazy." I watched for his sly grin.

"Sure, I did. Money can buy you anything, JT." The grin was beginning to spread. Sam sounded so confident of everything, even laughing about buying off the cops. I just couldn't believe this guy.

"Here's the ladder." Sam produced a paper bag from the back seat.

"Do you really expect me to use this thing, Sam?" I pulled the crazy contraption from the bag.

"Sure, it's easy. Just hook this end on your windowsill and gently lower the other end down the side of the house." Sam was holding the ends with the hooks.

"Sam, that's not what I mean and you know it. How can I sneak out? If my dad finds out I'll really be in trouble."

"Do you care? I thought you were mad at your old man anyway?" Sam kept pushing.

"Well, I am, but I still care." My emotions were so confused.

"Why? Doesn't sound like he cares about you or your old lady." Sam's choice of words angered me.

"She's not my old lady, she's my mom. I don't like anybody talking about my mom that way."

"O.K., O.K." Sam backed off.

"She's all right, she just gets a little crazy once in a while, but she's all right. Don't insult her, please." I didn't want to argue about my mother.

"O.K., I hear you. But your father doesn't seem to be any prize, so why stick around? Besides, you and I have big plans tonight." Sam's hand lightly touched my cheek and lingered for a second. Just long enough for my body to collapse into the seat and for my mind to erase every noble intention I ever had.

"What do you say, JT?" Sam's voice was soft and pleading.

"Well, maybe for a little while if I can get down that stupid ladder." I had to break the tension his touch had caused in me.

"Right," Sam said, laughing. "Here, I'll go over it once more for you."

Chapter 5

Supper was a disaster. Dad was in a terrible mood. First because of last night and second because Notre Dame had lost. Mom was quiet and withdrawn; I suppose she was still angry with Dad. Tom tried to start a conversation about the football game, but stopped when Dad yelled about the ignorant bastard who was supposedly quarterbacking.

I excused myself as soon as I finished and said I was going to my room.

At ten o'clock I went to the kitchen in my pajamas and robe. Tom had gone on a date, Dad was in front of the TV, and Mom was reading. On the way upstairs I said good night, and when I got in my room, I quietly shut and locked my door and quickly got dressed. It took five minutes to get my window unstuck, and another five to convince myself that I could climb down a flimsy rope ladder without crashing through the dining room windows. My fear of heights had returned in full force and just looking out the window almost made me sick.

Never before had I so blatantly defied my parents. I had never really been in trouble in school and until recently I had always gotten along pretty well even with my dad. But I kept remembering that slap and how devastated I'd felt when he accused me of being sneaky and dishonest. I knew if I kept thinking of all the negative things my folks had done I'd have a better chance of convincing myself to try my fate with a flimsy rope.

I finally got up enough courage to climb out the window and start down the ladder. My throat was dry, my knees were wobbling, and I was sure the shaking of my hands would cause me to fall. When I was almost down, I heard a loud whisper.

"Sweetheart, I couldn't do better myself, you're almost down." Sam was lounging against the wall with his hands in his jacket.

"Sam, what are you doing here? We're supposed to meet at the corner. What if someone sees you?" I was totally distraught.

"Never fear, I'll just tell them I'm trying to stop someone from breaking into a house, namely you." His hand reached out and I grabbed it.

"Thanks a lot. It's nice to know I can count on you when I need you." I jumped to the ground and secretly thanked God for the solid earth beneath me.

"Come on. My car is parked around the corner."

"What are we going to do now that I am officially a rotten daughter who has just defied her parents?" I asked on the way to the car.

"Now that you're down the ladder, the only way you can go is up." His clichés were too much. He continued, "We're going to celebrate your independence and initiate you completely into The World of Sam Bensen."

Something about the word *initiate* stopped me cold. But Sam just smiled and for some reason I wondered if I had on sexy underwear.

"Let me open the door for you."

"Thanks, but somehow that seems out of character for a macho man."

When Sam was in the driver's seat he answered, "JT, I love to do everything out of character. People in general are so boring." He started the car and we were off.

"Sam, I'm boring. Why do you want to go out with me anyway?" I couldn't believe I was actually saying this to him, but somehow I knew this was going to be a night to remember and Sam seemed in such an open mood.

"JT, you're not boring. You just think you are. Is

climbing out a window something a boring person does?"

"No, only a crazy person," I retorted.

"What would your pom-pom friend think of this?" Sam asked.

"Renee? She wouldn't believe it. I don't think I'd better tell her, either." I could just imagine Renee's response.

"Why not shock her a little? Her type needs a good jolt now and then."

"What do you mean by 'her type'?" By this time we were rushing down the expressway and I wondered where we were going.

"Oh, the prissy do-gooders who always make sure the teacher knows not only their name, but their social security number, dog tag number, and toothpaste brand."

"Toothpaste brand?"

"Yeah, you know what I mean. They just never stop talking about themselves or their family or their jobs or whatever boring thought that pops into their lifeless brain." I could tell Sam was starting one of his lectures.

"Hey, don't be so critical. Renee's my friend. You don't even know her." This conversation sounded familiar except the names had been changed.

"And I don't care if I do—she's got a good body, but that's about all."

"How do you know?" Why did Sam and Renee dislike each other so much?

"I can just tell. Besides I like giving you a hard time."

"Why?"

"Because I like to see those green eyes flash when you get angry or excited. You have great eyes. Did you know that?"

"No. No one except my mother ever talks about my eyes," I answered.

"If a person doesn't notice eyes, they don't notice

anything. Tell me, what color are my eyes? And don't peek, either." Sam turned his head.

"Brown, and I don't have to look. I noticed them the first day I saw you in Jakness's class." I knew I was right.

"See, you aren't boring at all. You noticed them first thing, huh? Well now, I officially welcome you to The Exclusive World of Sam Bensen." Boy, was I glad I had noticed his gorgeous eyes. But how could anyone miss them?

"You keep talking about this exclusive world of yours. Who else belongs?" My curiosity was getting the better of me.

Sam was smiling. "Nobody except you and me."

My heart pounded with excitement. What would this exclusive world of Sam Bensen's hold for me? "Say, where are we going anyway?" I asked when my heart slowed down.

"We're going to a place I know that plays a little music, serves a lot of beer, has a super pizza, and can be reached by using a nice private entrance and exit."

"You mean a bar. You're taking me to a bar? I'm not old enough." Now I knew Sam had gone too far.

"Old enough for what?"

"Neither are you."

"Neither am I what? See, your eyes are really jumping now. Are you getting excited or mad?"

"Sam, I don't believe you are really serious about taking me to a bar."

"You said you didn't want to be boring anymore."

"No, *you* said that. I'm beginning to think I was very happy with my boring life, safely hiding under the bedcovers in my room."

"JT, we have arrived."

"Here? I don't see a bar." I couldn't see any neon lights. All I saw were houses.

"Who said anything about a bar?" Sam stopped the car and opened the door.

"You did."

"Not me."

"You said a place that had music, beer, and food." I couldn't figure out what was happening.

"This is true, but I never said a bar."

"Oh, I just thought."

"Never just think. Always think through, around, in front of, behind. Then you'll never be bored—only amazed or surprised."

"Well, where are we anyway?" The area was certainly not commercial.

"My house. Come, you'll love the stereo, the refrigerator is full of beer, the carry-out pizza is right down the block. We'll go in the side door so no snoopy neighbors will see your lovely face."

"Sam, you're crazy. What about your folks?"

"No sweat. Dad is working."

"And your mom?" Sam had never talked about his family.

"No mom. She took off a couple of years ago."

"Oh, I didn't know. Gee, I'm sorry."

"Don't be, I'm not." He didn't seem upset at all.

"You don't mind not having a mom?"

"No, it was just a hassle when she was around. This way it's a lot quieter and my dad and I hardly see each other."

Sam bowed low and opened the side door. I walked in.

"It's sort of a mess," Sam apologized, "but it's home, sweet home."

"It's fine. You should see our house sometimes."

"Come on, let's sit in the living room. I'll get us some beers. You do want a beer, don't you?"

"Oh, sure, a beer is just fine." A beer is just fine, I thought, I can hold a beer can as well as a Coke, I guess. I had done it at Jeb's house. "So how do you get along with your dad?" I probed.

"Not bad, he doesn't bug me much. I can come and go as I please. He's even good about me getting in trouble at school. And somehow I seem to do a lot of that. Maybe it's my hair color, what do you think?" Sam was running his fingers through his hair, making it stand straight up.

"Yeah, I'm sure it's your hair. What *else* could it possibly be?" I made sure I had adequately exaggerated the *else*. Sam got the idea.

"Perhaps it's my cynical attitude. Somehow I just can't get serious about algebra equations and geometry problems. This is the age of the computer; nobody is ever going to use that stuff. Oh, maybe an engineer and maybe another math teacher, but for the rest of us it's a waste of time. If they spent time teaching us how to use a computer, now that would make sense. Do you understand what I'm saying?" Sam was trying hard to convince me.

"Sure, but what about the old idea that we need to learn the discipline of math and science?" I countered.

"Boy, they got you brainwashed, don't they?" He sounded disgusted.

"Well, I don't think you have to be so critical all the time. The way you talked about Jakness the other day I couldn't believe it." Who was he to call me brainwashed? My temper was starting to flare.

"Oh, Jakness deserves it. He doesn't know what side is up. All he knows is how to polish that red Corvette of his and how to keep the accelerator to the floor when he drives." Sam's temper was starting to flare too.

"Isn't there anybody at school you like?"

"Sure, you." For a second Sam's angry eyes stopped flashing.

"I mean teachers?"

"Well, certainly not Wilson or Jakness—that's for sure." Sam headed for the kitchen. "Time for another beer and I'm going to order a pizza. How's cheese, sausage, and mushrooms?" Sam was picking up the phone.

"Sounds great. Say, what time does your dad get home anyway?"

"Not for a long time. Are you nervous or something?" Sam was gulping the beer he'd just opened.

"You sure drink beer fast. You're not getting drunk, are you? I hate it when people get drunk. They're so obnoxious."

"Don't worry, JT, for you I'll switch to Coke when the pizza comes." Sam dialed the number and ordered the pizza.

When he was off the phone I asked, "How come you don't like Wilson?"

"Lots of reasons, I guess."

Sam didn't offer any explanations so I plunged right in again, "Did you really take a swing at him the other day?" I knew I risked making Sam angry, but I just had to know. The Sam that Tom, Renee, and half the kids at Lincoln described was not the Sam sitting in front of me. I had to convince myself that the real Sam Bensen was what I saw and not what the rest of the world thought they saw.

"Why are you so curious, JT? Does it scare you to think your date is a suspected felon?"

"No, I guess I just don't believe it and I want you to tell me the rumors aren't true. They aren't true, are they?"

"I'm sure they aren't. Rumors never are, or they wouldn't be rumors, if you get my drift."

"Well, did you hit Wilson?" I persisted.

"I don't know why you're so damn curious about it, but no, I didn't hit him." Sam's eyes told me to back off, but I didn't.

"What did happen? Something must have happened, or you wouldn't have been suspended." Since I'd gone this far, I kept on.

"Ever since I got expelled last year for that stupid bust, Wilson has been after me." Sam's words were rushing out. "Wilson was so mad last year when he couldn't find the grass I was supposed to be selling.

He wanted to get me kicked out of school for good but couldn't." His face hardened a little.

"I thought you *did* get expelled last year for selling drugs?" Now I was totally confused.

"I did get expelled, but only for a semester and it wasn't for selling drugs. I got kicked out for supposedly starting a fire in the bathroom."

"Oh, I thought it was for drugs." I was sure Brian had said it was a drug raid.

"See what I mean about rumors? Nobody in that whole stupid school knows what happened, but they sure do talk like they do."

I couldn't answer because I obviously was one of the guilty ones who had believed what I'd heard.

Sam continued, "For some reason Wilson thought we were smoking dope in the bathroom when all some of the guys were doing was having a cigarette. Anyway, when he came in one of the guys panicked and threw a lighted cigarette in the wastebasket and a fire started. I walked out of the stall about that time and Wilson thought I'd dumped something into the toilet. Just then he saw the smoke and since I was standing the closest he accused me."

"But if you didn't start the fire why did you get blamed?" None of this was making any sense to me.

"Well, JT, it's this way. The guy who started the fire was a big football jock and he wasn't about to own up and get kicked out, so I got the ax since I was standing right there and I'm a nobody in the sports kingdom."

"But that's not fair." I was furious by now.

"You got it, sweetheart. One valuable lesson in life: nothing's fair." Sam leaned back and took a long swallow of beer. Then he leaned forward and looked right at me. "You don't think I'm a pusher, do you?"

Sam's look was disarming and I wanted him to know how much I believed in him. "Of course not, it's just all the talk around school and then your trouble with Wilson. Sam, tell me what happened this time. Did you hit him?" I needed to fit all the pieces together.

"I told you I didn't hit him, isn't that enough?" Sam's eyes were blazing.

"No, if you didn't hit him I think everyone should know you didn't."

"Right! They should know I didn't hit him, but I promised the bastard that the next time he called me an 'ignorant dope pusher' I'd run him off the road. And if that didn't do any good, I'd smash his car into a million little pieces." Sam's voice had started softly, but it was getting louder.

"Sam, you didn't really threaten Wilson like that, did you?" I was afraid to hear his answer.

"You're damn right I did and I mean it, too. I've put up with that Wilson just long enough. He better stay away from me or he'll live to regret it."

I couldn't answer. My tongue wasn't functioning properly. I had no idea how to handle this violent side of Sam. It scared me.

Sam sensed my fear. "Oh, come on, JT, don't look so shocked. Nothing is going to happen. It's just that I get a little crazy sometimes. Come on, forget it, O.K.?"

Just then the door bell rang and Sam returned with a steaming pizza. We lost no time in devouring every bit of it. Sam kept his promise too and switched to Coke.

The pizza was gone, the stereo was playing low, and Sam and I were sitting quietly on the couch.

"I guess I shouldn't have pushed the issue, huh?" I looked at Sam, hoping to gauge his anger in his eyes. There was none.

"That's O.K. I'm glad you did. It feels good to talk about it. Jeb's the only one who knows what really happened. But let's forget about me. Let's talk about you. Are you glad you came tonight?"

"Yes, Sam, very glad." There was nothing else to say and I wasn't surprised to feel Sam's slightly moist lips on my neck. It was perfectly natural to look into his eyes and part my lips to meet his. He left burning sensations as his mouth moved gently from my neck, across my chin, to my eagerly waiting mouth. That kiss stopped all motion. I felt that this was what I'd been waiting for ever since I first saw Sam sprawled next to me in science class. As his hands ran through my hair and I leaned toward his chest, I knew all the trouble that was bound to come from sneaking out of the house was worth it. Sam and I were meant to be. My arms eagerly encircled him and I lost all thoughts except the one that I needed Sam and he needed me.

After a while I said, "Sam, I think I'd better get home."

Sam softly replied, "Yeah, I suppose so. JT, I'm so glad we met."

"Me, too," I murmured. The thought that I almost stayed home tonight was frightening. The thought that I had to sneak back in was suddenly more frightening. I was instantly on my feet and anxious to get going.

When I got home the rope ladder looked like too much to tackle. I decided to take my chances and go in the front door. I looked in the window and couldn't see any life. I slipped the key in and very gently opened the door. Sam's hand turned my head and our lips met for only a second. "See you Monday, sweetheart," Sam whispered.

I smiled and was through the door. Nobody was in sight when I paused to listen. As I hurried to my room, I heard the hall clock chime three times. Quietly I pulled the rope ladder in and hid it in the closet. I crawled into bed and fell asleep dreaming of Sam's moist lips and warm hands.

Chapter 6

Sunday found my dad in a slightly better mood, but Mom was still very quiet. I desperately hoped they still weren't angry with each other because of me. I was relieved that my escape and return had gone unnoticed. Yet I felt sad because I knew that since it had been so easy it would happen again until one time I wouldn't make it. I tried not to think of that. Instead, I remembered Sam's deep eyes, his touch, and my need to be cared about by him.

That night Renee called. "Hey, Jeannie, how's the grounding going?"

"O.K."

"We missed you last night. We had a great time."

"That's good."

"Hey, Brian says he can fix you up with a real cute guy as soon as you're not grounded. What do you say?"

"Thanks, Renee, but I don't think so."

"Why not?" When I didn't answer she pressed. "Is it because of Sam? Jeannie, are you serious about that guy?"

"Maybe, why?"

"But he's so much older."

"Renee, he's only sixteen."

"Well, he seems older, if you know what I mean. Can you handle that?"

"Oh, Renee, come on. We're not kids anymore."

"Yeah, but we're not adults yet either."

"Well, he says you have a nice body." In my desperation to say something good, I was afraid I'd blown it. After a short silence Renee answered.

"Sam isn't bad, either, Jeannie, but that's not the point."

"What's the point?"

"I'm not sure, Jeannie, but there's just something about that guy. You better be careful."

I wasn't sure what she meant. What was she trying to warn me about? "Don't worry, Renee, I'll be O.K. See you in school." I hung up wondering what Renee was trying to say.

The week passed quickly once Sam was back in school. He managed to control himself and made no snide comments at all. I avoided Renee all week, but on Thursday I bumped into her at the bus stop.

"How are you and Sam doing? I hear he's been keeping a low profile."

Renee was only trying to make conversation, but right away I got defensive. "How do you know what Sam's been doing? I didn't know you had any classes with him."

"I don't, but Brian does. Brian knows everything that goes on around here. Say, do you suppose your Friday night caper with him was a positive influence?" She was trying to keep the conversation light.

"I don't think Sam needs a positive influence." I really wanted to tell her I thought it was our Saturday night rendezvous that was influential, but I was afraid she might lecture me, first on sneaking out of the house, second on the dangers of hanging out with Sam Bensen, and third on the stupidity of going to a boy's house alone. I decided to shift the conversation to Brian. "Maybe it's Brian who needs a little positive work. He sure is a gossip, isn't he?" I couldn't resist that little dig.

"Brian isn't a gossip. He's just popular so he knows a lot of people and they tell him stuff. What's the matter with you anyway?" Renee was hurt. I could see the red creeping into her cheeks, but I wasn't up for a big argument with her.

"Nothing. Just forget it. See you later." I walked off. Boy did I walk off.

Then one night during one of our usual supper drills Mom commented, "I haven't seen Renee for a while. What's she up to these days?"

"She's very busy being popular," I quipped.

Tom added, "I see her with Brian Gardner a lot. Say, why don't you have her fix you up with one of Brian's friends?"

"I don't need to get fixed up. I can do just fine by myself."

"I know you can," Tom blurted. "I just thought maybe it would be easier."

"You aren't still interested in that jerk who kept you out so late, are you?" Dad chimed in.

"Dad, Sam is not a jerk." My defenses were up immediately. "You don't even know him and you're calling him names. Why don't you give the guy a chance?" I continued.

"I know the guy, Jeannie, and I agree with Dad. You can do better than him," Tom butted in.

"Maybe I don't want to do better. Besides, do you even know the guy, or do you know just what everybody says about him?" I answered sharply.

"I see him in the halls all the time," Tom answered.

"I didn't ask if you see him, I asked if you know him. Have you ever had a conversation with him?" Tom's attitude was driving me crazy.

"Not really. It's just that he has such a reputation that I feel I know him without talking to him."

Dad looked up sharply. "Oh, yeah, what kind of reputation does he have besides keeping girls out so late?"

"Nothing, Dad. Never mind." I wanted this conversation to end right now. I knew my face was turning red and suddenly I'd lost my appetite.

"Well, maybe we should meet him," Mom offered. Good old Mom coming to the rescue.

"Yeah, I suppose it really isn't fair to judge him without a trial," Tom admitted.

"I still want to know about his reputation," Dad persisted. "Tom?"

By this time Tom was getting uneasy too. See, he really isn't such a bad brother, it's just that sometimes he talks too much and can't seem to stop.

"Tom, I'm waiting," Dad snapped.

"It seems that Sam is well known for disagreeing with the teachers," I answered for Tom.

"What do you mean?" Dad questioned me. "There is nothing wrong with disagreeing. There must be more."

"He has a bad habit of disagreeing with more than his mouth," Tom answered.

"You mean he likes to fight?" Dad was quick to pick up Tom's meaning.

"Yeah, he got suspended last week for hitting Mr. Wilson, a math teacher who's been at Lincoln about forty years," Tom said.

"What, is this guy crazy or something?" Dad turned to me. "Jeannie, I don't want to hear that you're with this maniac ever again, you got that?" Dad was shouting by this time.

"He never hit Wilson," I yelled. "Tom, do you believe everything you hear? Did you also hear Wilson called Sam 'an ignorant dope pusher'?" As soon as I realized what I'd said I regretted it. Of course Dad picked up on it immediately.

"Oh, now I find my daughter is keeping company with a junkie. Just what I need, a daughter who is on drugs!" By this time Dad was raging. Mom tried to calm him down, but I was just getting warmed up.

"On drugs? Now you're accusing me of taking dope. You're incredible, you know that? You're the most bigoted, narrow-minded person I've ever met." I slammed my fork down. "First you call me sneaky, now you accuse me of being on drugs, none of which is even close to the truth!" I jumped up and knocked my chair over.

"Don't you yell at me!" Dad was on his feet and coming toward me.

"Don't you lay a hand on me." Suddenly I was calm and never before had I been so deadly serious. Something must have warned my father because he stopped. Mom stepped between us.

"Jeannie, don't talk to your father in that tone of voice, please," she begged.

"I'll talk calmly to him when he talks calmly to me." I was now speaking directly to my mother. I could hear my father's heavy breathing. "Please excuse me." I picked up my chair, walked quickly to the stairs, and ran to my room.

Somehow it seemed as if I'd been through all this before. I hated arguing with my parents, but they were becoming so unreasonable. If my dad would only think before he opened that dumb mouth of his. And Mom needed to learn how to stick up for what she knew was right. Tom could use brotherly lessons in how to aid a sibling.

I sat in my room and contemplated what life would be like for the next four years in this very insane house. Would graduation ever come so I'd finally be able to go away to college? I even vowed to study harder, so I would be sure to get into a school somewhere far from home.

About nine thirty Tom came to my room and said I had a phone call. I went downstairs and pulled the phone into the hall closet for privacy. I was so happy to hear that deep voice.

"Hi, what's up, JT?"

"Nothing. Nothing at all," I said, sighing.

"That nothing sounds like a big something to me." Sam read my voice.

"Just another big round here at the Tanger residence. And guess who was the main attraction?" I wanted Sam to know what was happening.

51

"Sounds like I was. Will I win an Academy Award?" Sam asked.

"No, I will. I'm sure my father is still in shock over my performance."

"Yeah, tell me all."

I filled Sam in on round number two in the battle of the family.

"Ah, JT, I'm sorry to cause you so much trouble. I'll make it up to you. I promise." Sam's concern made me smile.

"Let's just forget it. How about plans for this weekend? I think the ladder is getting rusty from disuse." Even though I was in the closet I spoke softly so no one would hear.

"Rope ladders don't get rusty," Sam said, laughing. "Does this mean you're asking me for a date?"

"It sure does." I couldn't believe I was asking him, but it felt so comfortable.

"Well, I accept." Sam's call made the world seem so much lighter.

When I got off the phone Mom asked if she could talk to me. We walked up to my room and Mom closed the door.

"Look, honey, your dad is under a lot of pressure lately. You have to understand that." Mom's voice was pleading with me.

"So are you, Mom, and you don't act like a crazy person." I hated it when she defended Dad.

"Your father is just very worried about you."

"Well, aren't you worried about me, too?" I wanted to trap her.

"Sure I am, Jeannie." Mom knew she was losing.

"You don't scream and rant and rave. Why does he?" I really didn't want her to feel worse, but I couldn't seem to stop. I suddenly felt sorry for her. I realized that she had no more control over Dad than I had over Sam.

"Let's not talk about Dad," I said. "What do you think? Would you meet Sam sometime? Mom, I know you'd really like him. You know, he notices eyes just like you do!"

"Then he certainly can't be all bad, can he?" Mom was grinning. "I get the feeling you're going to see him whether your dad and I approve or not."

"Yes, Mom, I am." Maybe I was crazy to tell her that, but I had to. "Mom, he's not like everybody says. Oh, sure, he's gotten into trouble, but the stories everyone tells aren't true."

"Most stories are just that." Mom seemed deep in thought, but at least she was listening. "What do you think will happen around here when Dad finds out?" Mom was really concerned. But it was apparent she wasn't going to tell him.

"I don't know, I can't think about that." My mind was just not ready to deal with that thought. "Maybe you could talk to Dad for me. You were always so good at it when I was little."

"Jeannie, that was a long time ago. Things change, you know." Mom was insinuating something.

"What do you mean?" I didn't like the tone of her voice.

"You're not a little girl anymore. Your battles are your own now. Your dad and I are having enough troubles of our own right now."

"Troubles of your own!" Mom never talked to me about her relationship with Dad or any troubles they might have.

"I don't want to burden you with our problems, but I'm sure it has been rather obvious lately." Mom was staring straight ahead.

"Yeah, I guess it has." When I thought about it, I knew it was true. But I'd been so wrapped up in my own problems that I wasn't aware of much else.

"Is there anything I can do?" I was beginning to sound like Mom now.

"No, Jeannie. It's something we have to work out. I just want you to know that I don't always agree with your father, but I can't fight your battles for you when I have my own to wage." Mom looked at me for just a second. There were tears in her eyes, but she was smiling. I was embarrassed, but I felt so close to her. She hugged me and then was out the door before I could say anything. My mind was reeling. What an exhausting day!

Chapter 7

Life settled down to a relatively trouble-free pace for the next month. The fall became our perfect time. Since Dad didn't get home until five and Mom a little after, Sam and I were free every day from three fifteen on. Tom worked after school at the grocery store so I didn't have to worry about him seeing us together all the time.

We would race out of our last-period classes and be out of the parking lot before most kids had gotten to their lockers. Lots of times we'd drive to the country. We spent day after day exploring every side road within a forty-mile radius. Often we would just stop the car, sit under a tree and talk. Sometimes we sat without talking, and the silence never seemed wrong or uncomfortable. We always managed to get back just in time for me to make it look like I'd been home for a while.

Mom never again mentioned her troubles with Dad and I wasn't about to bring up the subject. I really wanted to bring Sam to meet Mom, but every time I was about to say something to her I chickened out.

I used the rope ladder a lot while I was grounded, but as soon as I was free again I made up one excuse after another to get out of the house. I used football games, movies, or school activities as alibis. When I said I was going out with the girls my parents never questioned me as long as I managed to get home at a reasonable hour. Tom saw Sam and me together, I'm sure, but he never said anything to me or to Mom and Dad.

Sam was even holding his own at school. When

he got angry with Jakness, he managed to hold his tongue and with Wilson he mostly just didn't go to class. It had been a real freak of nature that he'd gotten Wilson for math anyway. The luck of the computer, Sam said. He'd decided his best attack was a failure in the class and then next year he'd just take a different math class. I didn't approve, but then it wasn't my decision. Sam went just enough not to get hassled for being truant and so far it had been working.

Jakness often tried to bait Sam, but most of the time Sam just laughed in the appropriate places like the rest of the class did.

One Monday morning late in October Jakness was in one of his angry moods. I wondered if he and his girlfriend had a fight over the weekend or if the principal had yelled at him when he started in on Sam.

"Bensen, what is the average life span of the monkey?" I could tell he was out for blood. He was frowning and pacing back and forth like he did when he was about to corner someone.

"I don't recall reading that fact," Sam responded.

"Well, what do you recall reading, if anything?" Jakness emphasized the last words.

"What do you mean by that?" If Sam sensed the trap, he didn't show it.

"Just what I said. What do you recall reading, or don't you read?" Sam was definitely his intended victim.

"Yes, sir, I read, but who cares about the average life span of the monkey? It really isn't going to help me earn a good buck, is it?" Why was Sam challenging him on a day like this?

"No, it probably won't, but knowing the average life span of the monkey just might give you some idea of how long you are going to live." That nasty smile Jakness had when he had clearly made a fool of somebody appeared on his face.

56

Sam was on his feet, "Listen, Jakness, your jokes are really sick, but you are sicker. Can't you think of anything better to do than insult students all the time?"

"I don't insult students, Bensen." The accent on "students" made the message loud and clear.

"And I don't insult teachers, so I guess that leaves me free to insult you all I want." Sam was frowning, and that hate gleam had come into his brown eyes. I wanted to tell Sam to cool it, I wanted to tell him to sit down, but I knew better. Sam would never forgive me if I interfered.

"Bensen, get out of here and don't come back. You're a troublemaker and I don't need it, or you." Jakness's face was turning red and he was breathing fast.

Sam just stood there ignoring Jakness's order to leave. He stared right at Jakness and said, "You people are all alike. You're all flunkies who can't do anything else, so you teach—or should I say 'try to teach'? Why don't you try getting a real job?"

"The only real job I would like right now is to throw you out of here, and now! Move!" Mr. Jakness slowly approached Sam. They were standing face to face. Sam had his feet firmly planted and his hands were in his jacket pockets. Mr. Jakness was leaning slightly forward, his hands at his sides. Suddenly his right hand shot out and he shoved Sam. As Sam fell against the desk and stumbled backward, Jakness said, "Stop harassing me, you stupid dope pusher! And don't try threatening me like you did Wilson. My Corvette will make mincemeat out of that piece-of-junk Volkswagen of yours."

Sam regained his balance, straightened his jacket, and turned toward the door. As he walked out of the room, I could see his clenched fist and tight-lipped mouth. I heard him moving quickly down the hall. I wanted to run after him, but I didn't. As a result, I didn't see him or hear from him for three days and

57

I was totally panicked. Those cold eyes and that determined stride had me convinced this incident wasn't going to be taken lightly.

The rest of that class was a blur. How could Jakness get away with taunting and even pushing Sam? I wondered if teachers got expelled, too. Sam sure would have if he had pushed Jakness.

All day everybody seemed to be ignoring me. Maybe it was my imagination, but I really doubted it. The conversations either stopped or got very quiet when I came into a class. I knew they were all talking about Sam and Jakness. Why does everyone love to talk about the bad things that happen rather than the good?

Renee made it a point to catch me after school. I'm sure all she wanted to do was remind me of how right she was.

"I hear Sam Bensen, your good friend, really did himself in today."

"What do you mean?" What could I possibly say to save Sam?

"I can't imagine a student comparing a teacher to a monkey," Renee stated.

"You obviously have your facts wrong. Sam didn't do the comparing, Jakness did." I could feel my patience leaving fast.

"Well, that's not what Brian told me." Renee was so defensive, I just wanted to scream at her.

"Brian wasn't even in class. I was, and I heard it all."

"Maybe you only heard what you wanted to hear, Jeannie. Jakness is a teacher. I doubt if he'd start on Sam."

"Well, he did."

"Maybe you were high and didn't hear it right?"

I was speechless. Why would Renee say something like that? She knew I wasn't into drugs. Was this my old friend talking to me?

"Renee, you know I don't do things like that." My voice was a whisper.

"I don't know anything about you anymore, Jeannie." Renee shook her head and then said very quietly, "Every time I try to talk to you, you take off. Ever since you met Sam you've changed and I don't think it's been for the better." Just then Brian appeared at Renee's side. "I want to help you, Jeannie."

"Help me? Then believe me instead of him." I motioned toward Brian and stormed off. What was happening to me? What was happening to my friends? All the way home these dreadful questions haunted me. How could Renee, who had known me for what seemed like forever, think I would smoke marijuana or pop pills or do any of those things? Why did everyone think the worst of Sam? Nobody knew him at all. Why were we both being condemned by everyone?

Home life hadn't gotten any better either. Dad was on another rampage. I secretly wondered if men had bad times of the month too. First Jakness and now my father. I made a mental note to question my mother about the life cycle of males the next time I had the opportunity.

"Where the hell is your mother? I work all day and I have to come home to an empty house. She should be here to eat with us." Dad was muttering as he buttered a slice of toast.

"Dad," Tom said calmly, "I told you she phoned and said she had to wait for an important call from a judge. She said she'd get home as quickly as she could." Usually Tom had a way of calming Dad down. Tonight I wasn't sure tact was the solution to Dad's dilemma.

"A call from a judge, huh! That hotshot lawyer she works for should take his own calls. I hate the idea of your mother being someone else's personal servant."

Yeah, I thought, you just want her to be yours.

God forbid she should wait on someone else like she does you. What a hypocrite!

"She'd better be home soon, or I'm going to go down there to see what's happening. Enough is enough!" He took a bite of toast and chewed furiously. I'm sure he couldn't even taste it through his anger.

Tom added quietly, "She'll be home shortly, Dad. Why don't you go on in and read the new *Sports Illustrated?* It's lying right by your chair." Dad finally nodded and left the kitchen.

"Dad sure is uptight these days, isn't he?" Tom asked as he got the hamburger ready.

"He treats Mom like me. He's always bossing her around." Disgust was apparent in my voice.

"Yeah," Tom responded, "but he isn't all bad, you know. Sometimes I get the idea you really don't like him."

"He's all right, I guess. He just drives me crazy sometimes. I don't like the way he acts sometimes toward Mom and me. It's like he doesn't believe we can take care of ourselves. He doesn't do that to you, though." I bit into an apple as Tom started making the salad.

"No, not really. I suppose it's because I'm a man or at least a member of the male species. I guess Dad feels more protective when it comes to you and Mom."

"I guess Dad really believes that stuff about male superiority and male protectiveness. Do you, Tom?" I was sitting at the kitchen table watching Tom work.

"Not really. Some poor jerk who was jealous of his wife's competence probably started all this male-female rivalry." Tom smiled and his eyes flashed. For a brother, he wasn't too bad at times.

"Say, are you still interested in Sam Bensen?" Tom asked as he walked to the refrigerator.

"I still like him, if that's what you mean," I said.

"I heard about the trouble he got into. What was

that all about anyway? Was Jakness doing one of his usual numbers?"

"Yeah, he started giving Sam a hard time."

"What happened? I heard Sam got mad and called Jakness a monkey?" Tom raised one eyebrow. "Actually, that isn't a bad comparison when I think about it," Tom said, laughing.

"Wrong, Tom, Sam didn't call Jakness a monkey." Tom had obviously heard the wrong story too. "Jakness told Sam if Sam knew the average life span of a monkey then he'd have some idea of how long he'd live."

"Oh," Tom said as he sat down at the table with me, "so *Jakness* did the insulting, not Sam, huh?"

"That's right." At least Tom knew the true story if no one else at school did. "And not only that. Jakness pushed Sam into a desk and Sam never laid a hand on him. Then Jakness told Sam to keep his car away from his fancy Corvette."

"It figures. I think Jakness has a love affair with that car of his." Tom shook his head. "Anyway, the whole thing sure is too bad. Sam's reputation makes everything he does into a full-scale incident."

"I know. Just associating with him seems to have sealed my fate at school. It just doesn't seem fair." I was getting so depressed thinking about it.

"Maybe, Jeannie, it would be a good idea if you started dating someone a little less controversial in the eyes of the teachers and kids." Tom was trying to be kind, but I wasn't interested.

"No, Tom, I'm going to stick with Sam. If I quit him now I'd only be admitting what the whole world seems to be saying."

Tom shrugged and started unloading the dishwasher.

Mom came in as we were just getting everything ready for supper. "Mom, can I fix you a drink?" I asked. She looked pretty tired.

"Thanks, no, Jeannie," Mom replied. "I had a drink with Paul."

Just at that moment Dad barged into the kitchen. "Oh, now it's 'Paul'! What happened to 'Mr. Dillon'?" Dad's tone of voice was accusatory.

"Oh, Al, I've worked for the man for six months now. Don't you call your boss by his first name?"

"Yes, but that's different," Dad retorted.

"How is it different?" I knew I should have stayed out of it, but as usual I stuck my whole leg right in up to the hip.

"It's different, because I'm a man and my boss is a man. Besides, it's none of your business anyway, so butt out." Dad was getting hotter by the second. He turned back to Mom.

"What were you doing at a bar with 'Paul' anyway?" Dad continued, putting big emphasis on the word *Paul*.

"We weren't at a bar, we were at the office and we were waiting for a call from a judge about a subpoena. Didn't Tom tell you I called?" Mom was anxious now.

"Yes," I chimed in, "Tom told us but Dad obviously didn't believe it."

"Jeannie, this is none of your business so stay out of it." Dad was really angry, but I didn't care.

"Let's eat," Tom said. Good old Tom, always one to try to keep peace in the family.

"Good idea," Mom said. "I'm sure you're all starved. Thanks for waiting for me."

"That's O.K., Mom, we don't mind waiting for you." I tried to give her one of my loving smiles; she looked like she'd had a rough day. I could see the wrinkles around her eyes that often appeared when she was tired.

"Well, I mind," Dad cut in. "I mind a lot. Supper here is at six o'clock and, by God, I want everyone here when it's time to eat." Dad banged his knife down.

"We've waited for you lots of times. Leave Mom alone. Can't you see she's tired?" Why did I have to challenge my father when I knew better?

"Jeannie, I've had just about enough from you. What I say to your mother is none of your concern. So shut up or leave."

This time I heeded the warning and left. I didn't feel like eating anyway. I hated to leave Mom with him in that kind of mood, but then I figured she would be all right since Tom was there. After they finished eating, I could hear them arguing for a long time. I sure didn't remember them arguing like that when I was little. How come I kept thinking so much lately about what it was like when I was young? Even grammar school seemed far away. It had been so easy when all I had to worry about was what I was going to play at recess, or who I was going to walk home from school with.

Chapter 8

After two days Sam still hadn't come back to school and I was getting frantic. He seemed to have just disappeared. I was so desperate I found Jeb after school on Wednesday. "Have you seen Sam around? I really want to talk to him."

"You're JT, right? You're the reason I haven't seen much of Sam this fall." Jeb's hair was falling in his eyes.

"Yes, I'm Jeannie," I answered. "I'm so worried about Sam. I haven't seen or heard from him since he got into that hassle with Jakness."

"That science teacher is really something. I'd like to find out where he lives and pay him a friendly visit some night. Or maybe I could leave him a message written into a broken windshield on his car. Hey, that sounds like a great idea. What do you think?" Jeb was grinning widely.

"Jeb, do you know what you're saying? You better be careful about who hears you talking like that." I was frantically looking around to see if anyone had overheard our conversation. Thank goodness we were on a busy street where the cars were plentiful and noisy.

"JT, you really are as straight as Sam said. I can't believe he's hanging out with someone as innocent as you." Jeb seemed surprised that I was so worried. "But then you are beautiful and Sam always has excellent taste when it comes to the women," Jeb said, laughing.

I could feel my face turning red. I tried to get back to the question of Sam. "Jeb, have you seen Sam?" I asked.

"I can see you really don't know Sam at all, do you?" I shrugged my shoulders. "When Sam gets angry nobody sees him, nobody talks with him, and if a person is smart he doesn't even try." Jeb sighed.

"Where does he go? What's he doing?"

"Sam gets himself a bottle or two, finds a private spot and drowns himself in liquor," Jeb answered. "There's no talking to him when he's like that either."

"Do you know where he is?" I persisted. I was shocked and scared by Jeb's remarks.

"Not really. I have a few ideas, but I'm certainly not going to look for him. He'll return when he's ready. When he's in one of his moods, I stay far away. You aren't thinking of trying to find him, are you?" Jeb asked.

"No," I lied. "I guess not. I suppose I'll just wait until he comes back to school. Thanks anyway." I turned and left as fast as my feet would go without breaking into a full-speed run. Jeb's remarks were too much. I needed time to think all this through. Oh, Sam, where are you?

I went home and locked myself in my bedroom. I just wasn't up to facing my family right now. Dad had been unusually quiet the past few days. After our battle we mostly ignored each other. Mom seemed preoccupied whenever she was home and Dad buried himself in front of the TV. I didn't want Mom to see I was upset. She might decide to talk with me when what I really needed was time to think.

I kept going over the things Jeb had said as well as those he implied. "Nobody talks to Sam...nobody bothers him...he gets a bottle or two...he'll return when he's ready."

I kept remembering the angry spark that sometimes shone in Sam's eyes when he was disturbed. I recalled his very bitter sarcasm when he talked about Wilson. Was Jeb right? Was it better to steer clear of this sometimes crazy person? No, this was my

Sam, and he needed me. I wanted to defend him and help him, too. That remark about the bottles had me upset too. Lots of times on our after-school jaunts Sam would stop and get a six-pack, but he never seemed to get drunk. A couple of times when he picked me up on a Friday or Saturday night he smelled like he'd been drinking, but it never seemed out of control.

Jeb seemed to know a lot about Sam that I didn't. Oh, I knew that on occasion Sam's moods changed when he was drinking, often he was so funny and other times very withdrawn, but he'd never done anything to make me suspect that he would hide behind liquor. The more I thought about it, the more I was convinced that I was Sam's only hope. Once I had convinced myself that I was his savior, I realized the next step was to find him so I could begin my saving. If only I had heeded Jeb's very good advice and left Sam alone.

After supper I told my parents I was going to study at Renee's house and left. I figured that was a pretty safe lie because I knew Renee wasn't about to call me. We barely spoke when we met in the halls so I didn't figure she would choose this evening to renew our fading friendship. At the corner I caught a bus to Sam's house.

I wasn't sure what I'd say to Sam or his dad, but I did know I wanted to talk to Sam face to face. All the way there I rehashed my words. Finally I gave up. I hoped the words would just come once I knew Sam was all right.

When I got there, I could see a faint light in an upstairs window, so when I rang the doorbell, I figured somebody was at home. Nobody answered and I was sure I'd heard the bell ringing inside the house. I tried again and waited impatiently.

"What do you want at that house, young lady?" Startled, I whirled around to face a very small, old woman standing three feet from me. She looked as if she had just stepped out of a 1930s photograph.

"I'm here to see Sam," I responded. "Do you know if he's home?" It was none of her business what I was doing, but at this point I was desperate for any type of information I could get.

"Of course he's home. He's been in there for a couple of days now. I keep hearing that awful music playing and his car is in the garage." This old lady was a real sleuth; I hadn't thought to check the garage for his car.

"Oh, thanks." I turned again to ring the doorbell. "I wonder why he doesn't answer the door then?"

"He probably can't find it," she snapped.

"What do you mean?" Immediately I felt defensive.

"Young lady, are you a friend of his?" The old woman's gray eyes were questioning.

"Yes, a good friend." I was going to be sure she understood.

"Then you should know what's going on in there." The old lady obviously knew more than I did.

"What exactly do you mean?" I was beginning to wonder what I did know about Sam.

"If you're such a good friend you should know that the Bensen men all solve their problems the same way, with their hot tempers, their bottles of booze, and their biting tongues. Why do you suppose Mrs. Bensen took off?"

"Well, I really don't know. I guess it's none of my business."

That last remark had no effect and the informer continued, "Well, I can tell you. She just had enough of those two fellows. Her husband spent his time at the tavern down the street and the son hasn't been any better. Like father, like son, they always say, and it certainly is true in this house. Why do you want to see Sam anyway? You certainly don't look like any of the other kids that come around here. Oh, that boy with the long blond hair bothers me."

Must be Jeb, I thought. "You can't judge a person by his hair." I could see that profound statement had a lot of effect. Why didn't Sam just answer the door so I could escape from this woman?

"He isn't going to answer the door, so you might as well leave." She seemed so sure of herself.

"How do you know?"

"Because I've been ringing his doorbell for two days and I get no answer. Kids these days are so rude. I hope you aren't like that."

Then I knew why Sam wasn't answering the door. He probably figured it was this crazy old lady and I didn't blame him.

"Is Mr. Bensen home?" I figured I might as well get all the information I could.

"No, he works nights. He won't be home until morning. That is, if he comes homes at all. I suspect one day he'll disappear just like his wife. How people can be so irresponsible is just beyond me. He just has no control over that boy. Imagine letting a boy drink and not go to school every day. I don't know what this world is coming to."

"Me, either." Maybe if I agreed with her she would leave, and Sam would let me in. I should have known better. Finally I decided this was useless. "Well, good night. I'll come back some other time." I turned and fled down the driveway. The old woman was still talking to herself as she went into the garage next door.

I'd spotted a drugstore on the corner a couple of blocks away and decided to call Sam. Maybe this time he would answer. At least I knew he was home, but I was still scared. What if something terrible had happened to him and he wasn't able to answer the phone or come to the door? Maybe he had fallen down the stairs. Maybe there was a gas leak in the house and he had been asphyxiated.

I fumbled in my purse for twenty cents and dropped it in the money slot. I dialed and waited. There was a busy signal. Maybe his dad was on the phone—no, the old woman said he was at work, so that meant Sam had to be on the phone. I dialed again, this time it rang and rang—I lost track after eighteen, but I was determined to let it ring until Sam answered. I was trying to send signals through the phone telling him it was JT. Finally there was a click, but no voice.

"Sam, it's me, JT. Talk to me please." There was another click and the line went dead. I desperately dug in my purse for two more dimes. I just had to talk to him. This time the ringing stopped after two tries. "Sam, don't hang up, please! I'm so worried about you. Are you O.K.? I want to see you. I was afraid something happened to you." I was talking as fast as I could—anything to keep him from disconnecting the line again.

"What the hell do you want anyway? Do you get your kicks out of hanging around with weird people? Take a hint, kid, and find some other freak to entertain you!" It was definitely Sam's voice, but the tone was sarcastic, bitter, and cruel. My mind was whirling.

"What are you talking about? Sam, I'm your friend." I jumped in before he had a chance to continue his tirade.

"You're not my friend. What do you think I am? Stupid, like your other friends? This is Sam Bensen, and Sam Bensen has no friends, and needs no friends. Take a walk, sister. Get a pom-pom and join the rest of the Lincoln High kids as they parade around trying to play at life, sweetheart."

His use of the word "sweetheart" had none of his old affectionate meaning. This time it was a dirty word, cutting me like a razor. "I just want to help."

"Well, you can't help. Nobody can. Just leave me alone." Sam sounded hurt and angry.

"I can't leave you. I care about you!" I pleaded with him to listen.

"Ah, bullshit. You're just like the rest."

"Sam, I'm not, just give me a chan—" I never got to finish the sentence. I was interrupted by Sam's ranting and raving.

"Don't ever call me again. Go back to Lincoln High and tell them for me I shall have my moment of sweet revenge. That bastard Jakness has been on my case all year. This time he went too far. The minute he laid a hand on me it was all over. You tell them for me, never again will Sam Bensen be so humiliated!" He slammed the receiver down. I stood in the phone booth in a state of shock. I couldn't even raise my hand to put the receiver back. My chest felt like it had been hit with a baseball bat and my head had become a battleground of enraged feelings. I heard someone talking to me. The drugstore man was replacing the receiver.

"Are you all right? Is there something I can do for you?" He was propelling me out to the counter. I gratefully leaned against it.

"No, thanks, I'm O.K. I have to leave now." I buttoned my jacket and slowly walked toward the bus stop. I must have gotten on a bus, but I don't remember it, or the ride home. My only thoughts were of Sam and what he'd said. Did he hate me? Was our relationship over? Were the wonderful times of these last few weeks going to be washed away with tonight's cruel words?

Chapter 9

I woke up to the smell of toast burning and the sounds of my father's cussing. For a brief instant I prayed I had only dreamed about last night's nightmare with Sam, but I knew only too well it was a fact of my life. Sam had cut me out. He had done everything he possibly could to insult me and get rid of me. He had also promised to have his revenge. What was I going to do? I was fourteen years old, and I wasn't sure I could handle this alone. But who could I turn to? My ex-best friend was certainly out of the question. Tom would never understand my involvement with someone he considered a loser. Some kids at school talked to the social worker or counselor when they needed help. But I couldn't just walk in cold and spout off about how wonderful Sam Bensen was. Sam had promised revenge and the school—Jakness in particular—needed to be warned. Just thinking about relaying Sam's message was absurd. None of the teachers were what one could call the sympathetic type either. The only person who might be a possibility was my mother. Lately she seemed preoccupied, but maybe it was worth a try the next time I had the opportunity. With that bit of hope I got out of bed.

My first-hour science class dragged by. All I could think about was the conversation with Sam. Conversation was the wrong word—a humiliating putdown was a much better description of our telephone exchange.

Jakness unexpectedly asked me to stay for a second after class. He seemed reluctant to say what was on his mind, but then asked, "Jeannie, have you seen

Sam lately?" He was looking at me so intently, shock must have registered on my face because he quickly added, "Well, I heard you were his friend and I just thought maybe you'd seen him."

I recovered enough to want to know, "Why are you interested in knowing if I've seen Sam?"

"Well, Sam hasn't been in school since the trouble we had and if he doesn't come back we'll never get it straightened out." He looked nervously at my science book.

I couldn't believe what Jakness had just said. "No, I haven't seen Sam since that day in class." Well, I wasn't exactly lying because I had only talked to him, and not seen him.

"Jeannie, if you do see him, will you tell him I was at fault and I'll do what I can to help him out when he comes back." Jakness seemed to be pleading with me, his voice subdued.

"Sure." What else could I say? I picked up my books and left the room. I spent the rest of the day trying to make some sense of the last twenty-four hours.

That evening I decided to talk with Mom. She could listen without judging. For a change Mom was home on time and Dad was in a good mood at the supper table. When supper was almost finished Dad asked, "Margaret, what do you say we go to a movie this evening?" He was smiling.

"We haven't been out in a long time. What made you think of that?" My mother was smiling, too.

"I was just thinking that it definitely has been too long. Let's go as soon as we're done eating so we can catch an early movie. Maybe we can stop somewhere afterward, too."

"But, Al, it's a working day tomorrow!" Mom reminded him.

"That's O.K., tomorrow is already Thursday so we'll survive." Dad was eager to go. He quickly finished his supper. "What do you say, Margaret?"

"Sure, why not? I'll be ready in a few minutes." As Mom got up from the table she glanced at me.

"Jeannie, is anything wrong? You look pale." Mom put her hand on my forehead.

"No, I'm O.K. It's just that I wanted to talk to you tonight."

Mom was immediately concerned. "Is something wrong? Are you having problems at school, Jeannie?"

"No, not really. I just wanted to talk, that's all." I tried to smile. I didn't want Dad to start asking questions.

"Jeannie, why don't you talk to your mother while she's getting ready? I'll get the car out of the garage. Tom, will you see to cleaning up this supper mess?"

"Sure, Dad," Tom answered.

"Come on, Jeannie." Mom was heading up the stairs, so I followed.

When we were in the bedroom Mom asked, "What's up, hon? Something I can help with?"

"I don't really know." I couldn't think of a way to start. I knew Mom was in a hurry and Dad would soon be honking the horn.

"It's about Sam Bensen," I began haltingly.

"What about him?"

"Well, he got into some trouble at school and I want to help him." I knew there wouldn't be time to go into great detail.

"What kind of trouble is he in?" Mom asked.

"He got into an argument with Mr. Jakness and walked out of class a few days ago. He hasn't been back since, and the fight wasn't even his fault. Mr. Jakness himself said so this morning."

"Have you talked to Sam since this happened?" Mom was busy trying to find a pair of slacks to wear.

"Yeah, last night," I said with a sigh.

"What did he say?"

"He told me to mind my own business. But I know

he didn't mean it, Mom." I was trying to convince myself as well as Mom.

"Why do you think he didn't mean it?" Mom slipped into a blouse.

"Because I know Sam, and he needs help even if he doesn't admit it." Why was I so sure of what I was saying?

Dad was honking the horn and I could tell Mom was getting nervous. "Dad's ready—I'm sorry, Jeannie, but I have to go. I guess you'll just have to do what you think is right." Mom started out the door. "Jeannie, let's talk about this some more tomorrow, O.K.?" She came back into the room and gave me a hug.

"Sure, Mom." What else could I say? Why did Dad have to pick tonight of all nights to want to go out? I was more depressed now than ever.

"Have fun," I called after her as she hurried out the door.

I was struggling with my algebra when the phone rang. "Jeannie, it's for you," Tom yelled from the hall.

As I walked to the phone I wondered who it could be. I didn't have many friends lately, so I couldn't imagine who'd be calling me.

"Hello." I'm sure my lack of enthusiasm came through very clearly.

"Hi. Meet me at the usual corner in fifteen minutes." There was a click and through my shock I realized I had just spoken with Sam. Or should I say Sam had just spoken to me? I was standing in the hall staring at the phone. I guess I thought if I stood there long enough the voice would return.

"Is something wrong, Jeannie?" Tom was standing in the kitchen door.

"No," I answered quickly and hung up the receiver. I didn't want to tell Tom who had called. I started to go upstairs.

"Hey, Jeannie, who was that on the phone? You

look like you've just heard from a ghost." Tom was following me.

I turned to Tom and smiled. "Just a guy from school. Say, I'm going out for a while, O.K.?"

"On a weeknight?" Tom was concerned. "I'm not sure Mom and Dad would want you going out without their knowing."

I smiled sweetly. "Oh, come on, Tom. Don't play big brother on me now. After all, you suggested not so long ago I start hanging around with some new kids." I was hoping he would simply presume the call was from someone he didn't know. I turned and flew up the stairs before he could ask any questions or give any advice.

I changed my sweater, grabbed my coat and purse, and rushed out the door. I kept hearing Sam's voice. He didn't sound angry, or was I just imagining that? Maybe he was furious with me for calling him. Maybe he'd found out I'd been at his house. I kept trying to push the nasty words he had said to me out of my mind. Maybe if I didn't think of them I could pretend Sam hadn't said them. I got to the corner in four minutes flat and realized that I was still ten minutes early. Just what I needed, more time to worry! What if those stories about Sam being crazy were true? Should I get into the car with him, or just turn around and get home as fast as I could? The longer I stood on the corner the more nervous I got. What if he didn't show up? Maybe it hadn't been Sam on the phone. Oh, where was he? My desire to see Sam had almost disappeared when I saw a green Volkswagen screech to a halt in front of me. Sam swung the door open. "Hop in. Somebody with your looks and great body isn't safe on the streets this time of night."

Sam was grinning his old grin at me. "Say, do you always meet people on the corner when they call?" When he looked at me and smiled, I had to laugh. I couldn't believe this was the same Sam I had talked to last night. One part of me was still hurt and angry.

The other part was so happy to see Sam and see him smiling that I decided to hide my hurt.

"Only if I know they are certified perverts," I quickly responded, "and your voice was definitely a class A pervert!"

"JT, you're getting good with the comebacks. I'm proud of you." Sam pulled me toward him and kissed me lightly on the cheek. I didn't know what to do. I was so glad to be with him, yet I kept remembering his angry words last night. But Sam's angry, cruel attitude seemed to have completely disappeared. Was Sam just going to ignore everything? Should I say something? More than anything I wanted Sam to stop the car and talk to me, but I didn't have the nerve yet to ask him to do that.

"Did you have trouble getting out of the house?" Sam was speeding down a busy thoroughfare.

"No, my folks went out, so I just told Tom I had plans."

"Did Tom know it was me who called?"   —

"No, why?" Why was Sam concerned about my family all of a sudden?

"Just in case we don't get home too early I don't want your family to come looking for me."

"What do you mean 'if we don't get home too early'? Where are you taking me?" I sat up straight and stared at Sam.

"Hey, JT, don't get nervous. Boy, you're really paranoid about me, aren't you?" Sam was driving even faster.

It was now or never, I decided; awful as it might be I had to find out what was going on in Sam's head. "Wouldn't you be a little paranoid if you were me? After all, our last conversation wasn't exactly friendly." I waited for a reaction, but Sam looked straight ahead and said nothing.

Then we were in the country, turning down a side road. It was dark and I wasn't sure if we'd ever been here before. We bumped along for about a hundred yards and stopped beside a grove of trees.

We just sat in silence for a long time. I kept hearing what I wanted to say in my head, but it just wouldn't come out of my mouth. Finally Sam broke the silence. "JT, I'm sorry about everything I said to you on the phone." The words came spilling out of him. "Sometimes I get crazy and I say and do some really awful things. I, I really am sorry. I don't know what else to say." He gripped the steering wheel and hung his head.

I didn't know what to say either.

Sam turned and looked at me. "You're the first person that I can talk to about so many things. You're so special." He reached for my hand.

My anger had long disappeared, but the hurt still lingered. I had so many questions to ask him, but I didn't know how to ask.

"Tell me what you're thinking. I need to know."

"Oh, Sam, I was so scared. I was afraid something had happened to you and then I'd be all alone again."

"Nothing happened. I'm O.K., see?" Sam sat up straight and turned his head from side to side.

"I was afraid you were mad at me because I called. I'm sorry. I didn't mean to make you mad. I was just so worried."

"Don't apologize," Sam interrupted. "You don't have anything to be sorry about. I'm the crazy one. Sometimes I just do these terrible things, it's like I don't have any control over myself. It's so frightening."

"Have you ever talked to anyone about this?" I didn't think he had.

"No, I'm always too ashamed afterward." Sam seemed to be confessing from somewhere deep within himself. He held my hand tightly.

"Does it only happen when you're drinking?" I looked straight ahead, but I could see Sam flinch.

He let go of my hand and started playing with the steering wheel.

"What makes you think I was drinking?"

"That crazy old lady told me you were. Who is she, anyway?" I suddenly wanted to get off the drinking subject.

"Who are you talking about?"

"That lady I saw at your house before I talked to you on the phone."

"You were at my house too?" Sam was staring at me now.

"Yes, didn't you know that?" I couldn't believe he hadn't heard the doorbell.

"No, I didn't know you came over." Sam's voice trailed off.

Sam didn't say anything so I continued, "Who was that lady? She sure is snoopy."

"You must mean Mrs. Hansen. She's always nosing around. What did she tell you?" The question Sam asked was casual enough, but there was something in the way he asked it that made me very cautious.

"Oh, not too much. She talked a little about your family, that's all."

"She obviously mentioned what boozers we are, or you wouldn't have asked about it. She's such a gossip. What did she say about my ol' lady?"

Sam's inquiry about his mother surprised me. "She just said something about her leaving, that's all." I didn't want to tell Sam what else she had said or hinted at. "Why did your mother leave anyway, Sam?" Since he'd brought the subject up I felt I had to know the answers to these questions before I could really understand Sam. Sam drummed on the steering wheel and said nothing. "I shouldn't have asked that. Forget I ever brought it up. It's none of my business."

Sam laughed softly. "Oh, JT, you worry too much about making me mad. I'm starting to believe that you care about me, even though I'll be damned if I know why. So I guess it's about time I filled you in on my life."

"Sam, you don't have to tell me anything if you don't want to."

"But I do. I want to tell somebody, and you're certainly the best sucker I know to get a little sympathy from, so just listen, O.K.?" His mocking tone didn't cover his hurt.

"O.K." I settled comfortably into Sam's side and rested my head on his arm. A Volkswagen isn't exactly the most comfortable place, but at that moment who cared? I had Sam and he trusted me. What more could I ask for?

"Mom and Dad never did get along very well. I remember when I was little. They were always arguing, so I used to stay in my room a lot. They never did anything to me—I mean they never hit me or anything. It's just that I couldn't stand to hear them fighting all the time, so I retreated to my room and played a lot."

"What were they fighting about?"

"I didn't know at the time what was going on, but now I think I have it all figured out. Dad never quite seemed to make it home with the paycheck. It seems he always made a few stops at the bars on the way home and by the time he got home the money seemed to have disappeared."

Sam sighed and settled back on his seat. "Now, don't get the idea that my dad is a bad guy, he's really a nice guy. That's the problem. It wasn't just that he drank the money away, lots of times he lent the money to his friends and, of course, they never remembered to pay him back. It hasn't changed much since Mom left either. He still doesn't bring his paychecks home very often."

"What do you live on?" I kept thinking of all our bills and how Mom and Dad were always worried about not having money to pay for them.

"We don't really need a lot. The rent is pretty cheap, and our house isn't exactly a palace. You know that old lady, Mrs. Hansen? Since she owns the house she thinks she has the right to know everything that is going on inside it. But she's not all bad. She feeds me sometimes. Mostly though she gets excited when Dad goes on one of his binges."

It crossed my mind that the binge she was concerned about was Sam's and not his dad's, but I didn't dare interrupt to say that.

"Well, I guess my mom just got fed up one day and left. I think it had been coming for a long time, but she just kept hanging around and being miserable. At the time, I didn't understand and I really hated her—but I don't so much now."

The thought of my mother leaving me made me sick. How could Sam be so casual about his mother's leaving? "Do you know where she is?"

"Yeah, she's in California."

"Why didn't she take you with her when she left? If your dad drank a lot and didn't have enough money to survive on, wasn't she afraid to leave you?"

Sam didn't answer for a while. His forehead was creased and he was deep in thought. I felt bad that I'd asked a question that obviously upset him. Finally he answered, "Who knows? Some day I'll find her and ask her just that. I did ask Dad that once and he said he figured Mom left me because she thought I'd be the one thing that could make my dad keep on living. Since he had me and the responsibility of taking care of me, he wouldn't become a skid row bum and give everything he owned to some needy friend. Maybe he's right. See, my dad is really a good guy, and I think he loved Mom. He just couldn't handle her life-style. She wanted a nice home and security. Unfortunately, that just isn't for my father. He was depressed for a long time after she left, but he always tried hard when he thought I was feeling bad. You know, not once since Mom left has he ever said anything bad about her. That's something, isn't it?"

"It sure is." What could I say? I just couldn't picture life at our house without Mom. Dad would be a raving maniac. My heart went out to Sam. I was beginning to sense what made Sam so unique.

"So that's the story of my mom, and I'm sure Mrs. Hansen must have said something about her, because she liked my mom and thinks Dad is kind of a bum." I just nodded. "I've found out a lot from her about what went on when I was little. She's a gossip, but one of the few gossips I know who usually has the facts correct."

I kept wondering if Mrs. Hansen had the facts right about Sam's drinking. I wanted to know, but I couldn't think of a good way to bring the subject up again. Finally I decided to just plunge in. After all, all Sam could do was leave me stranded out here in the country, but I knew he'd never do that to me. Or would he?

"Sam, Mrs. Hansen gave me the idea you do some pretty heavy drinking too when things get rough."

Sam just sat in his seat and never moved a muscle. "As a matter of fact," I continued, "Jeb sort of gave me the same idea. Now I know it's none of my business, but I'm worried." Sam didn't say anything, so I went on. "And the way you talked to me on the phone, too, really scared me. I thought maybe some of that behavior was because you were drunk."

After that long speech I decided maybe if I were smart I would just open the door and start back to town. That way I would save Sam some effort. Finally Sam turned and looked at me. At that moment, he looked so sad and so alone that I reached over and put my arms around him. I could feel Sam's body slowly respond to mine, and soon he was holding me very tight. "JT, I guess old lady Hansen is right and I suppose Jeb knows more about me than I want to admit, but please let's drop it. Some time we can talk about it. Right now, I just want to forget that horrible conversation we had. It's all I can think about since it happened. You don't know how sorry I am about the things I said to you. I was like a crazy person. Please forgive me."

Sam gently pushed me from him so he could look at me.

"Sam, it's O.K. I'm not mad at you anymore. Let's just forget what happened and go on from here."

"That's pretty hard to do, JT."

"I know, but at least we can try." Just then I remembered the conversation I'd had with Jakness. "Besides, Jakness said you should come back to school, so that's a new beginning right there."

"What?" Sam was incredulous.

"Let me tell you what he said."

When I was finished, Sam was puzzled. "That Jakness is up to something. I don't trust him. There is something very strange about that guy. I knew I shouldn't have argued with him that day. But I was so mad at him, I just wanted to smash him. At least I had sense enough not to."

"It's over now," I reminded him. "Are you still mad at him?"

"I don't know. Besides, what's the difference? I don't feel like punching him, if that's what you mean, and it's a cinch I'll stay away from him and his precious Corvette." Sam was lost in thought. His legs were stretched out under the steering wheel and his curly hair was all messed up.

"What do you mean 'stay away from him'? Aren't you going back to school?" I couldn't imagine another week of school without Sam.

"I don't know. Right now everything seems so complicated. Even though the argument was started by Jakness, I know I'll be blamed for some of it." Sam put his head back on the seat and sighed.

"Maybe not. Jakness said it was his fault. He'll be on your side rather than against you. That should help, shouldn't it?" I was so afraid Sam would just give up.

"Yeah, I suppose so. What are the kids saying about me? I just hate it when they all gawk at me like I was a prize rooster or something."

"I didn't know you cared about what the kids thought." Somehow I had never realized Sam worried about what others said. My surprise must have been obvious because Sam quickly responded.

"I don't really—but I guess I do. After all, I do go to the same school." Sam glanced at my grinning face. "Are you disappointed in me because I care?"

"No, I'm not disappointed, just surprised. You always act so unconcerned. I thought you liked to be different." Suddenly I realized Sam was just another kid having as much trouble growing up as me—maybe more. For a second I was terribly disappointed—my gallant image of Sam was fading. But when I looked at him I realized how much he wanted me to like him for what he was, and not what I thought he was. His eyes searched mine once again for acceptance and I responded in the only way I knew how. My hands gently brushed his hair as I whispered, "Sam, I love you." Somehow I always thought that if I ever said those words, my emotions would zero in on the word *love,* but this time I knew the *you* was the most important part.

A shy grin began spreading across Sam's face. The dimple in his chin deepened and I put my finger in it and laughed. "Don't ever change," I added. My eyes lingered on his lips and then moved up to meet his soft gaze. His eyes showed relief, thanks, and desire. I felt his warm hands on my cheeks. Our noses were touching and Sam smiled.

"Don't you ever change, JT, because I love you."

Nobody, besides my family, had ever said those words to me before, and I was so happy Sam was the first. I was certain this was the best first love any two people ever had.

Chapter 10

We drove home in silence. So much had been expressed we both felt drained. The silence was comforting, and I didn't want to ruin it by asking Sam if he'd be in school tomorrow. I decided to just presume he would. At the usual corner Sam stopped at the curb.

"Good night, Sam." I squeezed his hand as he kissed me.

"JT, thanks," was his only response. I watched as he drove slowly around the corner.

I realized it was cold standing on the corner and I turned and ran for the house. I was glad Mom and Dad's car wasn't in the driveway, so I knew they weren't home yet. Good old Tom had left the porch light on for me. With so much to think about I was sure I'd never get to sleep. But the next thing I knew the alarm was ringing and it was morning.

At breakfast Mom said, "Jeannie, I'm sorry we couldn't talk more last night. Let me drive you to school and we can talk on the way."

Her statement surprised me. Why did she want to talk? Then I realized that only fourteen hours earlier I had been desperate to talk to someone. Couldn't she tell how much I'd changed since last night? I thought love was supposed to be transparent.

"That's O.K., Mom, I feel better today. Besides, I know you like to get to work early." I was hoping Mom would get the idea that everything was all right. I didn't want to tell her about last night, especially because I'd gone out without permission.

"Are you sure, Jeannie?" She was looking right at me. "I'll be happy to go to work a little late."

"Mom, don't worry about it." I buttered my toast and changed the subject. "Did you like the movie?"

"Yes, it was fine. It was nice to spend some time with your dad." Mom was playing with her cereal. I had the idea she was indirectly trying to tell me something more.

"Has Dad left already?" I asked.

"He left about half an hour ago. He had an early union meeting." For some reason I noticed how blue her eyes were.

"That strike business must be over, huh?" I hadn't heard Dad mention it lately.

"It looks that way." Mom's short brown hair always looked so soft. It bounced when she talked. "Maybe your dad can relax a little now."

"Maybe you can, too." I couldn't resist the remark. Mom just smiled and shook her head.

"Jeannie, sometimes you're too perceptive for your own good."

I didn't really know what she was talking about, because all I could think about was Sam. I was having a hard time keeping my mind on the conversation.

"Right." I laughed; I walked over and kissed Mom on the cheek. "See you at supper, Mom. Bye."

I was nervous all the way to school. I kept hoping Sam would drive by and pick me up. I wanted the chance to see him before he went in to face Mr. Jakness. Maybe I could give him a little moral support. I didn't see him though, and finally slipped into my desk before the bell rang. Jakness was a stickler about being late and I didn't want to put him in a bad mood in case Sam showed up.

All through the class I alternately watched the door and the clock. I hoped Sam would come through the entrance before the bell rang and yet at the same time I wanted class to hurry and end. Finally, I gave up hope when there was only five minutes of class left. I was bending over my pile of books on the floor when I saw a familiar pair of Nike running shoes pass right in front of my face. At the same time I heard Jakness come to an abrupt stop. I jerked back in my seat and after what seemed a very long pause I heard Jakness.

"Well, good morning, Sam."

"Good morning."

"After class I'd like to see you for a second, O.K.?"

"Sure." Sam's voice was clear, confident, and soft as he tried to settle into his seat without drawing attention to himself. Yet every face in the room turned to look at him. I just wanted the bell to ring so Sam could be spared those curious looks. I could feel my own face burning as I tried to hide my own obvious emotions. When I couldn't stand it even one more second, the bell finally rang. I turned to Sam. He was looking directly at me.

"Good morning, JT. Are you sick or something? Your face is flushed."

I just wanted to slap that silly grin from his face. He knew exactly why I was blushing. "I'm fine, thank you." I could feel my face burning even more. As the rest of the class moved out of the room, I started to leave, but Sam touched my arm.

"Hey, what's the hurry? Don't you want to see the show?" He winked at me and his eyes were dancing.

I didn't know how to respond. The arrogant, confident Sam Bensen had returned. Had I only imagined last night? Was the Sam Bensen I'd seen then only another actor in the drama of his life? No, I knew no one, not even Sam, could act that well. Last night was real, today was the acting. But it didn't upset me; we all have to act sometimes and maybe Sam had to act a little more than the rest of us. I liked both Sams—because I knew they were really one.

"Do you want me to stay?" That he asked me to seemed a public declaration of his caring for me.

"Of course. You're the only reason I'm here, you know." Sam's smile faded.

"I hope not. I hope you're here for yourself first." Sam had to care about himself or else it wouldn't work. Before Sam had a chance to respond, Jakness interrupted.

"Sam, I think you and I need to get what happened the other day straightened out."

"Whatever you say." Sam wasn't helping the situation at all. I kept looking out the window, wishing I were somewhere else.

Jakness started for the door. "Let's go down to the assistant principal right now and get all this over with, O.K.?"

Sam looked at me, shrugged his shoulders, and said, "Sure, why not? That office is getting real familiar to me. See you later, JT." He followed Jakness.

As they left the room Jakness turned back to me, "See you tomorrow, JT." Great! Now even the teachers were calling me JT. I sighed and headed for my next class.

By lunchtime I still hadn't seen Sam. I was worried, but I was afraid to ask anyone where he was. Renee was sitting with Brian munching on potato chips when I walked by her table.

"Hi, Jeannie," Renee said. I paused, wishing I could talk to her like I used to. She must have sensed my reluctance to move on. "Want to join us?" Renee ventured.

"Yeah, Jeannie, come on." Brian moved over.

"Thanks," I said as I slid into a seat opposite the door so I could watch for Sam.

"So how's everything going with you two?" I figured a lead question like that would send Renee into one of her monologues and I would be free to watch the door in case Sam came in.

"Pretty good." Renee smiled. "Say, did you hear Brian is running for the student council?"

"Oh, no, I didn't. Uh, good luck, Brian," I stammered. As Renee told me about the election I couldn't help but notice how much she'd changed since the summer. Her tan was completely gone and her skin was soft and light. Her blond hair had been recently cut and it brought out her high cheekbones. Her blue eyes were sparkling as she talked about Brian and the election; she looked so much older and so much better. I briefly wondered if I had physically changed, too. My mind just wasn't concentrating on Renee's words.

"So what do you think?" Renee asked.

"I think you look real good, Renee. I like your haircut."

The shocked look on her face was almost funny. "Jeannie, what are you talking about? Haven't you heard a word I've said?"

"I just wanted to tell you how great you look." I quickly took a bite of my hot dog. Maybe if my mouth was full I wouldn't have to talk.

"Well, thanks, I'd like to say the same for you, but you look awfully tired and worn out. Is everything O.K.?"

The sincerity in Renee's voice brought my eyes from the door straight back to Renee. She had that old questioning look that I remembered so well. She did know me, even if we hadn't talked in so long. I wanted to tell her everything, I knew she would understand eventually. But just then Brian had to ruin it all.

"I suppose she's worried about Sam; he's been in the assistant principal's office all morning I hear."

My thoughts of confiding in Renee were pushed aside. If Brian, the school gossip, knew something about Sam, I wanted to know. In my most nonchalant tone I inquired, "Oh, really, do you know what's going on?"

Brian just smiled and said, "Let's ask Sam himself—here he comes."

I turned and saw Sam approaching from another entrance. He sauntered across the cafeteria, winding his way through the tables. A few kids said hello and then a voice from the back yelled, "Hey Sam, seen any monkeys lately—other than Jakness, that is?" There was a ripple of laughter and I turned to see Jeb. "Anyway, man, we're glad you're back. Are you here to stay?"

At that question everyone got quiet waiting for Sam's answer. Sam grinned and said, "Of course I'm here to stay, and wait until you hear about what's happening tomorrow." He picked up an apple from a table and tossed it to Jeb, who caught it and sat down. By this time, Sam had reached our table and slid into the chair across from me. He said hello to Brian and Renee, then turned to me.

I couldn't help noticing how his tan shirt made his brown eyes look so dark, and how his tight blue jeans hugged his body. His hair was in the usual disarray and I just wanted to run my fingers through those soft curls. Sam had just spent the morning in the assistant principal's office and all I could do was admire his physical attributes.

My hands were resting near my plate and Sam reached over and grabbed them. "Smile, JT, everything's O.K." When he winked at me, I had to laugh. Clutching his warm hands calmed me considerably.

Brian leaned over and asked, "So what happened, Bensen? You always keep this school hopping, don't you?" His voice was both curious and condescending.

"The name is Sam, and like I said, tomorrow Lincoln High is in for a first—you'll find out like the rest, Gardner." Sam smiled pleasantly at Brian and then his attitude seemed to dismiss him.

Brian shrugged and said, "Renee, are you finished?"

"Not quite," she answered. Renee, for some unexplainable reason, was quiet. She looked at me and then at Sam. Finally she finished her milk and pushed her chair out. "See you later, JT." She walked off before I could answer. Never before had she called me JT. What had she meant? Before I could think much about it, Sam interrupted my thoughts.

"Now that we're alone, listen to what happened to me this morning." He leaned forward, talking softly so no one else could hear. "Jakness and I go down to the assistant principal's office and Reardon's busy so Jakness says to wait, he had to see about his next class. He told the secretary that I shouldn't see Reardon until he got back. So I sit there all period, and was I getting disgusted. I was ready to walk out of there about ten times. Kids kept coming in and out so I'm sure everybody in school heard I was sitting in the office." Sam glanced around to see if anyone was close enough to hear us and then continued.

"So anyway Jakness finally comes back and we go into Reardon's office. Right off Jakness starts talking and making excuses for me—actually more for himself—but he sure is getting me off the hook at the same time. So then Reardon asks me about the whole thing and I tell him what happened. I try to make it fast and short. Jakness was nervous and I can't figure out why." Sam's forehead was wrinkled from the frown he was making. "Then Reardon tells me to go out. So I go outside and sit. I'm dying to know what is going on. Pretty soon the principal goes into Reardon's office and then the phone panel lights up and the secretary wasn't making any calls so they were talking to someone. The whole period just about passes. Finally the principal leaves Reardon's office and I get called back in and this part you won't believe.

"Reardon says to me, 'Sam, tomorrow in class Mr. Jakness is going to apologize to you for what happened.'

"I look at Jakness and he's staring out the window.
93

I look back at Reardon and ask him why. He says, 'Mr. Jakness believes it's important that he apologize. Since we often make students apologize to teachers in front of the class, he feels it's only fair for him to do the same.'

"'Oh,' was all I could say. But then I started feeling bad and said, 'Hey, he doesn't have to do that—let's just forget it.' The thought of Jakness groveling just didn't sit right.

"Finally Jakness said, 'No, Sam, we can't forget it.' He was looking straight at Reardon, but Reardon was looking at me. Then he got up real fast and started to leave without saying anything more to me or to Reardon. It was strange. I was feeling real uneasy and I don't know why, so I said, 'Well, if you change your mind and don't want to do it, it's O.K. with me.' He just grunted and walked out the door.

"I looked at the assistant principal and he said, 'I guess you might as well go to lunch,' so here I am. Can you believe it? A teacher at Lincoln apologizing to a student, and Jakness of all people. He has embarrassed, humiliated, and ridiculed more kids, and to think he is going to apologize to *me* of all students."

Sam couldn't believe it and neither could I. "That's really something. I don't understand what's going on at all." For some reason the whole thing was making me very uneasy. Something just didn't fit. I didn't know what or why, but the idea of Jakness apologizing was very unsettling. Just then the bell rang and I pushed my chair out. "Sam, I have to go to class, see you later."

"I hope so. Hey, let's do something tonight, O.K.?"

"I don't think I can get out tonight. It's a week-night, you know?"

"How about the ladder then? Let's see if it's still usable."

"I don't know. You know how nervous I am when I have to climb down that thing."

"Please?" Sam looked so alone and I really did want to see him without all these kids staring at us.

"How about after school?" I asked.

"Can't. I promised my dad I'd help him. Come on, tonight...what do you say?" He looked so cute sitting there.

"Why not!" I finally agreed. "See you on the corner at ten o'clock." I knew trying to sneak out earlier would be too risky. "Bye." I turned and hurried down the hall so I wouldn't be late for class.

I could feel Sam watching me all the way.

Chapter 11

When I got to science class the next morning Jakness was already at his desk. Just as the bell rang Sam strolled in and sat down. I glanced at him and he winked.

Jakness got up slowly from behind the desk. He seemed nervous and I noticed sweat marks under his arms on the red shirt he was wearing. He looked all around the room.

"This morning, before I start class, I have a couple of things I want to say. I'd appreciate it if you'd put everything else away and just listen for a couple of minutes." He paused while books closed and pencils dropped.

Jakness continued, "Many of you were here last week when Bensen—I mean Sam—and I got into a little argument." I could see Jakness's foot tapping the floor. "Actually, it was more than a little argument—it was a pretty good fight." Jakness's face was beginning to get flushed. "Well, anyway, I just wanted to say to Sam in front of all of you that I'm sorry about what happened. It was my fault and I'm sorry, Sam." By the time Jakness finished, his face matched his shirt.

Everyone in the class was deadly quiet. No one said anything for what seemed forever. Sam was slumped in his chair, looking out the window.

"Bensen, I said I'm sorry." Jakness's angry voice cut through the air. Sam turned his head and looked at Jakness.

"I heard you. Apology accepted."

Jakness nodded and seemed to be waiting for

something else. When Sam remained quiet he finally turned to the blackboard.

"Today we're going to read pages 102 to 113." I heard the voice droning on, but I kept thinking about Jakness's anger. One minute he had been so nervous and unsure and the next he was back in control and angry. Maybe he had expected Sam to say more. Suddenly it dawned on me: he expected Sam to apologize to him, too. Then he wouldn't have looked like such a fool; it would have looked like Sam was to blame for the argument, too. I was beginning to know enough about Jakness's slick ways to make me nervous. I wondered if he'd try to get even with Sam.

When the bell rang, we all headed for our next class. Sam and I were barely out the door when we heard a voice behind us: "Way to go, Bensen, you really made a fool out of Jakness, didn't you?" The speaker laughed and walked away before we could reply. I turned to see Jakness staring at Sam. I felt a chill move through my body. Did Sam sense it too? He just stood there with his hands jammed in his jacket. Finally we both started moving silently down the hall.

When I came to the stairwell leading to my next class I smiled at Sam and touched his arm. "See you later."

"Yeah," was his only response as he walked away.

By the time I got to my next class a couple of kids were already talking about Sam and Jakness.

One girl was enjoying the fact that a teacher had apologized to a student. Another thought the whole thing was ridiculous.

I noticed that none of the kids talking had even been in science class and already the story was being distorted.

By lunchtime the story was all over the school. For some Sam had become a hero and Jakness the laughingstock of Lincoln High. Others felt Sam was way out of line and they were on Jakness's side.

It all made me feel terrible. I was just playing with my sandwich instead of eating when Sam came in. He slid into a chair beside me. "I just knew there was something wrong about Jakness apologizing, but I couldn't put my finger on it. That Jakness is really a sneaky son of a bitch, you know that?"

"What are you talking about, Sam?" I was confused.

"He was told to apologize. The SOB didn't apologize because he was sorry, it was to save his own skin. It seems one of the school board members heard about the argument and was not too happy with Jakness. It seems there have been other complaints about him and this was his only way out."

"Are you kidding?" What a shock! "How did you find this out?"

"Oh, let's just say I have a connection. Besides that, he expected me to apologize to him and then he would have been partly off the hook. I almost did, too. Now, I'm so glad I didn't. I hope I don't regret it though."

"Are you worried about Jakness trying to get even?"

"A little," Sam confessed.

I reached over and took his hand. "Me, too, but just try to forget about it. Maybe it'll all blow over in a few days. You know how quickly things change around here." I really didn't believe Jakness would forget, but I wanted to do something to make Sam feel better.

Just then Jeb walked over to the table. "Hey, Sam, I think you're a real hero, but I wonder if Jakness does? If I were you, I'd stay away from that Corvette of his—especially if Jakness is in it." Jeb slapped Sam on the back and walked away.

"I see Jeb is thinking the same way we are." Sam tried a weak smile. "But you're right. Let's just forget about it. Hey, what should we do tonight? Celebrate because it's the weekend?" Sam was trying to be cheerful.

"Sure, I'll tell my parents I'm going to a movie with some friends. That'll get me out of the house early. I'll meet you at seven, O.K.?"

"Yeah, sounds good." Finally Sam's smile wasn't forced. We finished lunch just as the bell rang.

That night I managed to get out of the house without any problems. Dad was busy watching some game on TV and Mom was reading as usual. Tom had left early on a date so I just said good-bye and was on the usual corner by seven o'clock.

The wind was really cutting into me. It almost felt like snow. It was still November, but I was freezing! Where was Sam anyway? He usually wasn't late, and I was getting worried. Here I'd only known Sam three short months and I felt like an overprotective parent. I went from anger to panic. Where was he? Did something happen? Why wasn't he here? Finally I ran into the drugstore and called his house. A muffled voice answered the phone.

"Yeah."

I didn't think it was Sam, but I wasn't sure. "Sam, is that you?"

"No, no, this is his old man." The voice was slurred. "Who is this anyway?"

"Oh, this is Jeannie Tanger."

"Who?"

"Jeannie Tanger. I'm a friend of Sam's. JT is what Sam calls me."

There was silence on the other end, and then, "Oh, JT. I've heard Sam mention you."

"Is Sam there?"

"No! He left awhile ago. I don't know where he went and I don't care, either."

What was he talking about? Suddenly it occurred to me. Sam's father was drunk. That's why his words were so slurred. He was trying to sound sober, but wasn't exactly succeeding.

"Maybe he'll listen to you. He sure ain't listening to me."

I didn't know what to say so I just said, "Maybe. Well, thanks, I'll call later," and I hung up. Now I was really upset. Just then I saw Sam's Volkswagen, or I should say I heard it, squealing around the corner. As I hurried out of the drugstore I saw the green bug racing down the street. His driving sometimes got me crazy; one of these days he wasn't going to make a corner. But I didn't want to think about that now. I ran out to catch him before he thought I'd left.

The car came to a screeching halt. I opened the door and jumped in. Even before I had the door closed, Sam stepped on the gas and we took off. One look at Sam told me something was terribly wrong. The car smelled of beer. Sam's hair was completely messed up, his shirt was half unbuttoned and it was hanging out of his jeans. He must be freezing, I thought. There was dirt all over his pant legs and running shoes. When I set my purse on the floor I saw all the empty beer cans.

Sam hadn't said a word since I'd gotten in and neither had I. He was barreling down the street and I wasn't sure if I was more scared, or angry, or both. Just then Sam turned sharply to avoid hitting an oncoming car, and I heard myself yelling, "What are you trying to do, get us killed?"

His immediate response was low and angry. "If you don't like the way I drive, get out."

"Well, I think I will. You're driving like a crazy person."

Sam slammed on the brakes and I thought I was going to exit through the windshield rather than the door. I braced myself against the dashboard for support. When the car finally came to a stop, Sam reached in front of me and opened the door. Without a word, I grabbed my purse and jumped out. I made sure the door banged extra hard when I slammed it. Sam got the message and left rubber on the street as he flew off.

I was standing in a street gutter, and I wasn't even sure where I was. My mind was whirling. I was angry with Sam because he left me, and I was angry with myself because I knew something was terribly wrong, and I hadn't helped at all. I started walking slowly down the street, hoping I was headed in the direction of home. As I walked, I tried to figure out what had happened. After about ten minutes, I realized a car was following me. My heart started pounding and my palms were sweating. Every horror story I had ever heard started racing through my mind. What was I going to do? Who even knew where I was or who I was with? Maybe I was mistaken? No, I knew I wasn't. Those headlights were definitely right behind me. Finally I turned around and there was the green Volkswagen inching its way along. I was so confused and angry by now, I just turned back and kept walking. Sam pulled up in front of me about one hundred feet, got out of his car and came around and stood blocking the sidewalk as I approached. I stopped in front of him and stared at his dirty shoes.

"Listen, I'll slow down. Come on, get back in the car." I looked up at him. I could smell the beer on his breath and his face was pale. Sweat beaded his forehead; his eyes were pleading.

"Come on." He gently took my arm and steered me toward the car. I let myself be led and I got in when he opened the door.

Sam drove calmly and quietly. Finally I couldn't stand the silence. "So what happened? I was freezing waiting for you and then when you came you were acting crazy."

"Let's just forget it, O.K.?" Sam was watching the road.

"No, let's not forget it. That's no solution. I want to know what's the matter. You've been drinking, too." The last sentence was clearly an accusation.

"So what if I've been drinking? What's it to you? First you criticize my driving, now my drinking. Boy, you're a real joy to have around. I don't need a mother when I have you."

"Listen, don't start on me. I've about had it with you. Here I am worried sick about you and for what? So I can almost get killed, then yelled at, and finally dumped in the middle of God-knows-where. I could be home getting all this crap, I don't need it from you. Just take me home. Then you can do whatever you want—get drunk, feel sorry for yourself, wreck your car—who cares?" I crossed my arms and stared out the window. I hoped I could hold the tears back until I got home. I had had it. Sam didn't turn the car though. He just kept going and I knew we weren't headed in the direction of home.

"I said take me home." I tried to make my voice as cold and unfeeling as I could.

"I will when I'm ready."

"What do you mean—when *you're* ready? I'm ready now!" Who did he think he was, telling me what to do? "I'm sick and tired of you deciding when, what, and where." By now I was screaming.

"Hey, take it easy. I'm sorry, O.K.? If you want to go home, O.K. Can't we talk first, though?" It took me a few seconds to let my angry brain decipher his words. When I looked at him, I saw some life in his eyes for the first time all night. His eyes were my undoing. They always were. I hesitated and then answered, "Do you promise to take me home when you're done talking?"

"Sure, if you still want to go then."

What could I say? He knew he had me. Slowly my anger started to disappear. I asked again, "So what happened?"

"I got in a fight with my old man," Sam began.

"I figured that. What happened?"

"What do you mean you figured that?" Sam gave

me a quizzical look and then I realized he didn't know I'd talked to his dad.

"I called your house while I was waiting and your dad answered."

"What did he say?"

"Not much. He just said you weren't home and then said something about how you don't listen to him." I decided to leave out the part about him not caring where Sam was. I really didn't think he needed that right now. I continued, "What did he mean about you not listening to him?"

"Oh, he had this stupid idea about me and school!" Sam slammed the palm of his hand on the steering wheel. "He wants me to apologize to Jakness. Can you believe that nonsense? Me, apologize to that jerk!"

It was pretty obvious Sam wasn't even considering anything close to an apology. "Why did your dad suggest that?"

"I was telling him about what happened in school today, and what Wilson said."

"Wilson? You mean Jakness." This was confusing.

Sam looked at me and then said, "Oh, that's right. I haven't seen you since lunch." He reached behind the seat and got a beer. I decided to just ignore it. I didn't want another yelling match. Besides, now we were really out in the country and I'd never get home.

"When I got to math class," Sam continued, "I was the main attraction. Some punk called me a jerk for giving Jakness a hard time, so I grabbed him. Just then Wilson came in the room and started in on me."

"What do you mean, he started in on you?"

"Wilson says to me, 'Causing more trouble, eh, Bensen?'

"I wanted to smash him. Instead, I let the punk go and sat down. Of course that wasn't enough for Wilson. He said, 'You may have made a fool of Jakness today and a fool of me last year, but never again! Your number is up, kid. Don't even breathe the wrong way or I promise you you'll be out on your ear and this time you won't be back because I'm going to personally throw you out, pretty face and all.'

"Do you believe that? If I'd said that to a teacher, I'd be out faster than it takes to write the dismissal form. But Wilson can get away with it, or so he thinks. Not anymore. If Wilson so much as touches me, I'm going to run him and his car into a deep ditch some night."

"Sam, you can't mean that!" I was frightened because for some unexplainable reason I was afraid Sam did mean everything he said.

"I do mean it. I've had it with that school and those teachers." Sam was taking great gulps of beer.

"Does that mean you're not going back to school?" My heart was beating very fast.

"No, I'm going back. I promised my old man. Of course, after the fight we had, maybe I won't have to keep my promise." Sam seemed to like that idea. "Come to think of it, Dad was pretty drunk. He probably won't even remember what we said."

"Do you really think he'll forget?" I had a feeling Mr. Bensen was going to remember everything.

"No, I guess not. He wants me to stay in school and I don't know why. I'm never going to make it there. All I ever do is get in trouble." Sam seemed disgusted as well as resigned to his dilemma.

Just then we stopped. We had made a complete circle and were back at Jeb's house, the place we'd come the first night I'd been with Sam.

"Come on, Jeb is having a party and I want to forget all my problems." Sam pulled a paper bag from the back seat. "Or did you want to go home?"

What could I say? The last thing I wanted to do was see a bunch of kids right now, but what choice did I have? It was pretty obvious from Sam's mood that what I wanted wasn't of importance. "No, I want to be with you tonight." If this was the only way I could be with Sam, then I'd do what he wanted.

Chapter 12

Sam and I walked into the same clutter as last time. Newspapers and cans were everywhere. A few pop bottles were around too. Jeb was leaning against the kitchen sink.

"Well, hello, if it isn't our local juvenile delinquent and his favorite girlfriend. Glad you could make it."

"How you doing, Jeb? Here, I brought you a few goodies." Jeb took the bag and emptied two six-packs of beer and a bottle of whiskey. For some reason I thought of Mrs. Hansen. Why did Sam have all this liquor? Was he going to get drunk tonight? Did Sam have more than a little drinking problem?

Sam took a beer and handed one to me. We walked into the living room and cleared a place on the floor near the couch. A few kids nodded to us and then continued their conversations. The party was still rather quiet. A few kids at a time were filtering in.

Tim, a guy I'd met last time we were here, came in with a couple of other guys I recognized from school. "Hey, Sam, how's it going?" He reached over and shook Sam's hand. "Thought you might be in jail by now."

"Not yet," Sam said, laughing.

Tim turned to talk with the girl on the couch and I whispered to Sam, "What's that all about?"

"Nothing, really. Tim's in my math class and he's not one of Wilson's favorites, either. I guess he thought I'd have gotten even with Wilson by now." Sam was turned from me and I couldn't see his face.

"Sam, you aren't planning anything, are you?" I touched his arm, hoping he would turn toward me.

"JT, I'm afraid it just might be destiny. Wilson

and I are bound to clash, and when we do, I plan on coming out the winner." Sam turned to me then, and his eyes told me how serious he was.

"Sam, you talking about Wilson?" Tim asked.

"Yeah, I was just telling JT here about Wilson's numbered days if he doesn't get off my case." Sam finished his beer and took mine.

"Great! Anything you have in mind for him I'm all for." Sam laughed at Tim's remarks and started downing my beer. "What about Jakness? I can't believe he actually apologized to a student—and to you of all kids."

Sam nodded. "Yeah, I was almost starting to believe that horseshit apology of his, and then I find out he only apologized because the school board insisted—what a jerk!"

"Yeah, I heard he picked on one of the school board's nieces once too often and has been in hot water ever since. Is that true?" Tim asked.

"I guess so. What I can't figure out is how the school board found out about his sick remarks to me."

"Who cares? It's about time people knew how crazy Jakness is."

"Yeah, I guess so. I do know he better stay off my back or one of these days he'll get his, too."

Sam's talk scared me. He seemed to be enjoying this conversation and especially the idea of revenge too much. I couldn't stand listening so I excused myself and went to the kitchen. I was secretly hoping Sam would follow me, but he didn't. The conversation in the kitchen wasn't much better. Every aspect of school was under attack—teachers, classes, administrators—no one or anything was immune. Jakness and Sam were another big topic of conversation. Most of the kids loved Sam's tough-guy act, but weren't convinced he'd get away with it. They were sure Jakness would try to get even. Their talk and Sam's threats had me worried sick. Was there no end to all this craziness?

Finally I decided to go back to the living room and see if I could get Sam to go home. I found him sitting in the corner of the living room with the bottle of whiskey in front of him. He smiled when I came in and took my hand when I sat down beside him.

"JT, I like you. Did I ever tell you that?" His words were slurred and his head kept dropping.

"Yeah, you did." I didn't know what to do. Handling drunks wasn't something I knew how to do. "Hey, can we go home now?" I just wanted to get out of that place.

"Sure, sweetheart, in a little while. Let's just sit here and talk a little, O.K.?" His voice got higher on the last words. "Did I tell you about my dad? I'm mad at him, you know." Sam kept shaking his head and trying to make the words come out clearly.

"Yeah, Sam, you told me. Now can we go home?" I was upset enough without the thought of getting in trouble at home.

"Sure, you can go home, but I don't think I'll go home."

"What good will that do?" Sam didn't answer so I continued, "Listen, Sam, if you don't get me home soon, it'll be all over for me. Let's go." I tried to take the whiskey bottle.

"Leave that alone!" Sam's voice was slurred and angry. He pushed my hand away and took another drink.

"JT, you might as well forget it. He's in no shape to drive anyway." Jeb was standing beside me. "I'll get you a ride home. He can stay here tonight."

Sam heard part of the conversation. "Jeb, old buddy, I like it here. I think I'll stay. You too, JT." He tried to pull me closer to him; I resisted and stood up.

Jeb turned to Tim. "Hey, can you take JT home? Sam's going to stay awhile."

"Sure, I'm ready to go, come on." Tim started toward the door. I didn't want to leave Sam there, but I had to get home.

"Sam, I'll see you tomorrow, O.K.?" I took off before he had a chance to protest.

"Hey, where you going?" I could hear Sam's voice, but I didn't turn back. I hurried out the door before I changed my mind.

On the way home Tim asked, "So tell me, JT, what's Sam going to do?"

"What do you mean?"

"I mean about Wilson and Jakness?"

"Nothing, unless they do something first. The way they're out to get Sam really disgusts me," I said.

"You don't think Sam is innocent in all of this, do you?" He turned to me with a look of shock.

"Yes, of course I do. Jakness is the one who started the fight, and Wilson has no right to threaten Sam like he did."

"That's true, JT, but Sam isn't completely innocent, you know. Now I'm not exactly a favorite with Wilson myself, but I sure as hell am smart enough to know when to quit. But not Sam. He loves to provoke Wilson, and if that isn't guilty, I don't know what is."

I didn't know how to respond. If Tim felt Sam was a troublemaker, what did the rest of the kids at school think?

"If I were Sam I'd steer clear of Wilson and Jakness, but I don't suppose he will. He'll probably make it a point not to avoid either of them. Why does he do that? Does he like to cause trouble?"

"No, Sam's not a troublemaker. You don't know him at all." Somehow it seemed like I'd made this statement a few times before.

"I know him well enough to know he goes out of his way to stir up trouble. People don't like that, you know."

"Tim, I don't know what you're talking about. Sam doesn't try to cause trouble; it just happens."

"Oh, JT, you aren't that naïve, are you? Boy, Bensen really has done a snow job on you, hasn't he? It's really none of my business, but if you're smart, you'll take a walk and fast, away from Sam Bensen."

"Well, I'm not going to," I snapped.

"Hey, I didn't mean to get you upset, I'm just trying to give you a little friendly advice. Sam and Wilson or Jakness or all three are bound to have it out. Oh, it'll be quite a show, but you can be sure in the end the teachers will win and Sam is going to be a big loser. So if you want to back a loser, go ahead."

Just then we reached my corner. "Just let me out here, Tim." He pulled over. "Thanks for the ride, but no thanks for the advice. I'm sticking with Sam. He isn't a loser, you just wait and see." I opened the door and stepped onto the curb.

"Whatever you say, kid, but just remember who told you first." Tim drove off and I walked to the house.

No lights were on, so I hoped I would be able to go in unnoticed. The car wasn't in the drive so Tom was still out. At least then the door wouldn't be locked. But it was. I started searching in my purse for the key, but had no luck. Did I forget it? I was so mad at myself. How was I going to get in without waking my parents? I looked at my watch, but it was too dark to see. It had to be close to one o'clock and I'd sure be in trouble if Mom and Dad caught me out this late again. I was surprised they weren't waiting up. Just then a car pulled into the driveway. Tom was home; boy what luck!

"What's the matter? Lock yourself out?" Tom was laughing.

"Afraid so. I'm sure glad you came along."

"Aren't you pretty late, little sister?" Tom was opening the door.

"Don't start that big brother crap with me." I shouldn't have been so sharp with Tom, but after the night I'd had, my mood wasn't the best.

"O.K., O.K. Here I come along and help you sneak in the house late and I get yelled at. What's the matter? Have a bad date or something?"

"Yeah, something like that. I guess I'm just tired, too." I walked past Tom and started up the stairs.

"Wow, do you smell like beer and cigarettes. Where've you been?" Tom grabbed my arm and stopped me.

"Out with some friends. Besides, it's none of your business. I didn't ask you where you were, did I?"

"No, but I'm not fourteen years old and I don't come home smelling like the local tavern." Tom's tone of voice irritated me. Enough was enough."Were you with Bensen again?"

"Tom, get off my back. Here I'm grateful Mom and Dad are asleep, and what difference does it make? You're just as bad as they are." I shook my arm loose and ran quietly upstairs. Would all this trouble ever end?

Chapter 13

The rest of the weekend dragged by. Mom worked all day Saturday, so Dad was in a terrible mood by evening. Supper wasn't exactly pleasant. Dad spent most of the time complaining about Mom never being home and asking her why she had to work so much. Mom tried to ignore him, but it's pretty hard to do that when he doesn't stop talking.

Tom totally ignored me, but at least he hadn't told on me, so for that I was grateful. I didn't hear from Sam all day. I wasn't sure if I was mad or glad.

All his drinking was bothering me, but his attitude scared me more. I was afraid Sam couldn't control himself when he was drinking. I kept thinking about what Tim had said. I vacillated between thinking he was right and thinking he didn't know Sam at all. Did Sam try to draw attention to himself? Did he provoke his teachers on purpose? My brain got tired from thinking about it all, so I finally propped myself in front of the TV and watched the Saturday night movie.

On Sunday the phone still didn't ring for me and I was getting anxious again. I had that same feeling in the pit of my stomach that I'd had before Sam had gone off on his last binge. I was determined not to call him, but I could feel my resistance fading. I decided to try to do some homework because I didn't want to call Sam's house again. I kept thinking that Monday I could find out something. Maybe Jeb or even Tim would know where he was. I was sitting in my room trying to read when Tom knocked. "Jeannie, are you busy?"

"I'm just reading. What's up?"

"I heard all about your friend Bensen, and I also heard you were with him on Friday night at a real drunken brawl." Tom seemed upset and nervous as he talked.

"What did you hear about Sam?" I thought maybe I could find out something new, although I was sure Tom's interest was in me, and not in Sam.

"Oh, the whole thing with Jakness and then about Wilson. Doesn't that guy ever learn? I thought you had better taste than him." Tom was shaking his head.

"I have very good taste." Secretly I was beginning to wonder, but I wasn't about to admit that to Tom. "Besides, why are you so mad at Sam? He didn't do anything."

"That's the whole point, Jeannie. He should have apologized to Jakness and the whole thing would have been over. Doesn't he know how to play the game?"

"Maybe he doesn't want to." I didn't want to fight about it. "I'm not sure what game you're talking about, anyway."

"Jeannie, the game of school, it's real simple. You don't make fools out of teachers, especially teachers who are insecure in the first place. Jakness apologized to Sam because he had to, and Sam should have done the same. It would have been a trade-off and the battle could have ended."

"Tom, it's all ridiculous."

"What about you at that party? I heard Sam was drunk and bragging about getting even with Jakness and Wilson."

"Yeah, I was at the party." I tried to ignore what Tom said about Sam's threats.

"Was he drunk?" Tom persisted.

"He was drinking, if that's what you mean."

"Were you drunk?"

"Oh, Tom, come on. Of course not, I wasn't even

drinking. Does that make you feel better, big brother?"

Tom just shrugged. "I heard Sam was really drunk and he promised to give everyone at Lincoln a show we'll never forget."

"So, if he was drunk, he'll forget it anyway. Everybody says crazy things when they're drinking."

"Sam isn't everybody, though. He does have a reputation for doing crazy things."

"Yeah, I know, but I wouldn't worry about him, Tom."

"It's not him I'm worried about, Jeannie. I want you to stay away from him."

"Tom, Sam is my friend and he needs me now."

"He's using you, Jeannie. He's not your friend; wake up and see what's happening."

"I know what's happening. Everybody is trying to get me to dump Sam, but I won't, I'm sticking with him!"

"Jeannie, if I see or hear that you're with him again, I'm telling Mom and Dad." Tom's jaw was set and I knew he was serious.

"Tom, you wouldn't!" I knew he would.

"I would and I will." Tom started for the door. "I'm sorry, Jeannie, but the guy is no good and you can't tell. I care about you, damn it, and if you aren't smart enough to take care of yourself, I will."

"Tom, all you're doing is interfering. Why don't you let me lead my own life? Stop trying to play parent." I kept my voice down so Mom and Dad wouldn't hear.

"I'm not playing anything. Stay away from Sam Bensen. He's trouble." Tom walked out and closed the door.

Everyone kept predicting doom. Maybe they were all right; maybe I should stay away from Sam. But I couldn't. Right from the first time I saw him in class I knew he was different from the rest of the kids, and I liked that. Was I using Sam to become the exciting, unboring person I wanted to be? I certainly didn't agree with everything Sam did or said, but was that important?

For Sam I had given up all my friends. It wasn't easy to admit, but I missed Renee. I missed her terribly. I missed laughing about silly things. I missed Friday night sleepovers where we discussed in detail every person we knew. I missed Saturday afternoon shopping sprees and Sunday morning bike rides. I didn't do those things with Sam. For a minute, I wanted to be the old, fun-loving, and, I guess, boring Jeannie I was three months ago! Maybe I really hadn't been so boring after all. How had Sam been able to change my life so much? How had I ever let him become so important?

For a moment I saw myself over the last three months. Gradually I'd shut out all the people in my life except Sam. I followed him around as if I were on an invisible string. Even when he was nowhere around, I was following blindly. Were the kids right? Did Sam provoke the teachers? Did he like to be noticed, even when it was negatively?

Then it dawned on me—did I care? I loved him, and I couldn't give him up. I loved his great sense of humor, his gentleness, and his special love for me. I loved his soft touch, his lips against mine. Maybe there would be trouble, but I didn't care. Sam and I were meant for each other.

Chapter 14

In science class on Monday morning Sam didn't make an appearance. I wasn't surprised, but I kept hoping he'd show up. I wondered if he'd seen his father. I wondered if he meant those loud threats he'd made about causing trouble at school.

On my way to my second-hour class Tom stopped me in the hall. I hardly ever see Tom in school so when I saw him coming toward me I knew something was up.

"Jeannie, I just heard Bensen was in the parking lot before school and had more for breakfast than cereal, if you get my message."

"Did you see him?"

"No, but my buddy Ray did and he wouldn't make up a story like that."

"Is he still there?"

"I don't think so. Jeannie, stay away from that guy. There's bound to be trouble and you don't need to be in the middle of it."

"Tom, I'm old enough to take care of myself. But thanks for telling me." I hurried off before I got a lecture.

My next class lasted forever. I couldn't concentrate at all. I was scared for Sam. Why would he come to school drunk? I thought he was smarter than that. He was bound to get caught. The kids probably wouldn't squeal on him, but if it was so obvious to the kids, it wouldn't take long before a teacher found out. After class I decided to try to find Sam. Maybe I could talk some sense into him and get him out of there.

Sam should have been coming from English, but

he wasn't. I then tried social studies, his next class, but I had no luck there either. Finally I went on to my own class. On the way I spotted Jeb. "Have you seen Sam?"

"No, not today."

"What about yesterday?"

"Yeah, he was at my house most of the day."

"Was he drinking?" I was almost afraid of his answer.

"Why do you want to know?" Jeb asked.

"I just do, that's all."

"Yeah, I'm afraid he was. He's upset about everything. I guess he didn't call you, huh?"

"No, he didn't." I turned my head. I didn't want him to see how upset I was. "I heard he was in the parking lot before school and he was drunk."

"No kidding. God, he's really crazy."

"Do you know if it's true?"

"I haven't heard anything, but I just came from a test so there wasn't much talking." Jeb started down the hall.

"Where you going?" I didn't want him to leave me.

"I'm going to check out that rumor. Any messages if I find him?" Jeb was moving down the corridor and I followed.

"I guess not."

"O.K., see ya." Jeb started to leave.

"Hey," I called after him, "I have lunch fourth hour. If you find anything out, will you let me know?"

"Sure thing." He kept going and I turned to my class. At this point math seemed so unimportant. I could hear myself echoing Sam's sentiments all hour: Who was ever going to ask me if I could do an algebra equation or figure out the sides of an isosceles triangle?

Finally, after what seemed like hours, the bell rang and I hurried to the cafeteria. But Jeb wasn't there. I'd been counting on him to find out something for me. I walked through the line and got a sandwich and a Coke. I didn't feel like eating, but I had to do something to keep my hands occupied. I sat down facing the door so I could see everybody who came in. Unfortunately, everyone could see me, too. I saw Renee a second too late. I looked right at her as she came through the door. She saw me too and to ignore each other would have been just too obvious.

"Oh, hi, Renee."

"Hello, how's it going these days?"

"O.K., how about you?"

"Same here." Renee started to sit down and then must have had second thoughts. "Is it O.K. if I sit down?"

"Sure." As much as I wanted to talk to Renee, I couldn't. How could I explain that I was waiting for Sam, who was probably drunk somewhere in school? But then maybe she knew already.

"Brian'll be here soon. We always eat lunch together, you know."

"Yeah, I know."

"Where's Sam?" Renee asked.

"I don't know," I mumbled.

"Oh, aren't you going out with him anymore?"

"Why do you ask that?" I was convinced she knew more than she was saying.

"I just thought that maybe after what happened this weekend you two might have broken up."

So she did know some of what was going on.

"What did you hear about this weekend?"

"Oh, the usual rumors about Sam, you know what everybody's saying."

"No, I don't know. Who's going to tell me rumors about Sam?" I was getting frustrated. "What did you hear?"

"Why are you asking me? You were there, you ought to know what happened. Or were you drinking, too, Jeannie?" Her question shocked me.

"You're really something, Renee. Before you

119

practically accused me of being on drugs and now you insinuate I'm a drunk, too. I can't believe it."

"I never said you were on drugs," Renee answered.

"Oh, just forget it," I snapped.

"No, I'm not going to forget it. You always change the subject or back off every time I try to talk to you."

"You don't talk to me, all you ever do is accuse me. I can get that from my dad; I sure don't need it from you."

"Oh, come on, Jeannie. We used to be friends."

I cut her off before she could say more. "You're right, we *used* to be friends."

"Maybe Brian is right, maybe there isn't any talking to you when it comes to Sam." Renee's anger was beginning to match mine.

"Brian, Brian, Brian. I'm sick of him. Can't you think for yourself? Does that idiotic boy do all your thinking for you now too?"

"Just leave Brian out of this!" Now she was really mad.

"You brought him up, I sure didn't."

"You start in on Brian and I'll do a number on Sam that you won't forget."

"You're always doing a number on him. What would be new about that?"

"Well, Brian would never leave me like Sam left you Friday, I know that!"

"What do you mean, left me Friday night? He didn't leave me anywhere."

"That's not what I heard. I heard he dumped you like a hot potato."

"Back to the old rumors, I see. You can't even argue without rumors." My arguments were no more logical, but at the time who cared?

"What did happen then, if Sam didn't leave you? Why did you go home with Tim, or is that a rumor, too?"

"No, that's not a rumor. Tim took me home because, because..." My voice trailed off. I didn't want to admit to Renee that Sam had been too drunk to drive me or too drunk to care. "He just did, that's all." All the fight and anger went out of my voice. I put my hands over my eyes and sank back in my chair. Renee should have sensed my defeat. She should have told me everything was all right. She should have told me she still liked me. After all that's what friends are for. But we weren't friends anymore, were we?

"All I know, Jeannie Tanger, is that Sam Bensen is going to get into a lot of trouble the way he is shooting off his big mouth. I heard he has threatened both Wilson and Jakness. He's never going to get away with something like that. Everybody says he was drunk and rowdy and bragging about how tough he is."

What could I say? Tom had told me the same thing. It seemed pretty likely all the rumors were true. I couldn't even say anything I hadn't even talked to Sam. Everybody else knew more than I did.

"Well, what about it?" Renee was waiting for me to answer, but I couldn't. "Aren't you going to say anything?" Renee sensed my defeat then. "Jeannie, it isn't your fault. Sam's the one causing all the trouble. Nobody's blaming you, yet, and they won't if you stay away from him."

Before I could answer Brian intruded. "Hi, Renee, hi, Jeannie."

"Oh, hi, Brian, where've you been?" Renee turned to Brian with relief as he sat down.

"I was outside. I'm surprised you weren't out there, Jeannie. Sam was putting on quite a show."

My heart stopped its steady beat. Sam was up to something and Jeb hadn't returned. I waited to hear the worst.

"What's going on, Brian?" Renee asked.

"Sam was entertaining everyone who would watch

with imitations of Jakness and what goes on in his science class. This morning's liquor has really loosened him up."

"Didn't any of the teachers stop him?" Renee asked.

"No, that Bensen is smart. He waited until most of them were at lunch to start. How come you weren't out there, Jeannie?"

"I wasn't invited." My remark made no sense to them, but it sure did to me.

"Oh, well, that Bensen is a real jerk, if you ask me. No offense to you, of course, Jeannie." Brian was so thoughtless. Or maybe he knew exactly what he was saying.

"So is he out there now?" Renee pressed.

"No, some of the teachers must have heard something was going on and when a couple of them came out of the building, Sam took off." Well, at least I knew he was gone. That was good anyway.

"He did promise to return though, and bring us more entertainment."

My heart stopped for the second time. Would there be no end to this craziness?

Brian kept right on talking. "Wait until Jakness hears Sam was making fun of him; he'll go crazy. I know those two are headed for a showdown. I hope I'm around when it happens."

How disgusting! Some people get their kicks in sadistic ways. Just then I saw Jeb coming toward our table.

"Sam wants to see you. He's waiting down on the corner of Van Buren and Cuyler," Jeb said as soon as he got to me.

"You're not going, are you, Jeannie?" Renee reached across the table and touched my hand.

"Are you coming?" Jeb pressed.

"Jeannie, it's almost time for your next class. Don't go."

Later I realized Renee had been pleading with me. But I didn't hear her asking; all I heard was that Sam wanted to see me. Without a word I got up and followed Jeb out of the cafeteria.

Chapter 15

Jeb slowed down once we were out of the building and I managed to catch up with him. "Is Sam drunk?"

"You'll have to be the judge of that." Jeb wasn't going to commit himself.

"I hear he was putting on quite a show in the parking lot."

"That he was. He does a great imitation of Jakness. I wish I'd of had a movie camera." Jeb was chuckling to himself. Just then he pointed. "There's Sam, see you later. Stay loose." He turned and walked off before I could answer. I ran to the car. It was cold and I hadn't bothered to get my coat. When I reached the car, Sam opened the door for me.

"Hi, sweetheart, glad you could make it. Hop in, let's go for a spin. Hey, I'm a pretty good poet, don't you think?" There was no doubt Sam had been drinking—and a lot.

"Why don't we go for a walk instead? Maybe it'll clear your head." I should have known better.

"And just what do you mean by that?"

"I mean I'm not sure you're in any shape to drive."

"I'm in grrrrrrrreat shape." At that moment he spun out of the parking spot, tires screeching as we left.

"Sam, would you slow down, please?" I was scared. I wasn't sure Sam had even looked as he pulled into the street. He didn't seem to hear me. "Sam!" When I looked up, we were in the middle of the street and a car was coming right for us. "Sam!" This time I was screaming, "We're heading right for that car!'"

"Have you ever played chicken?" Sam seemed esmerized by the oncoming car. I screamed once more and covered my face. I was sure the end had come. I felt my chest tighten and I could feel my fingertips pushing into my face. I kept waiting for the clash of metal and the rattle of breaking glass. I braced myself for the impact. Nothing happened! Soon I heard Sam laughing. "Hey, that was great! That guy is pretty good at it."

I ripped my hands from my face and realized the car in front of us was gone. "Good at what?" I heard my own voice responding to Sam's remark.

"At chicken. He didn't swerve until the very last minute. Good thing there wasn't a parked car on the street."

"What are you talking about? You almost got us killed!"

"It's a great game, don't you think? 'Or don't you think?' as the infamous, soon-to-be-sorry Jakness would say." Sam had slowed down as we headed down his street.

"That was a game? You did that on purpose?" I could feel my hands trembling.

"Sure! Certainly in your limited lifetime you've played chicken before?" Sam pulled into his driveway. "It's one of my favorite games. One of these days I'm going to play it with Jakness. Last year he said, 'Bensen, I hear you're pretty good at chicken. I was the best when I was in school. Too bad I quit playing.' Quit playing, nothing. That guy is going to play the game of his life! I wonder who will win?"

Just then Sam pulled into his driveway. He opened his door and went to the house. I didn't know what to do so I stayed in the car; I didn't know what was happening. I did know I was very glad to be sitting in a car that wasn't moving. My hands were still trembling. Sam was really crazy. We could have been killed. I should have been sitting in English class, but I was here instead. *I* didn't break the rules, *I* wasn't a troublemaker. What was I doing with Sam Bensen anyway? Finally I decided I was going back to school. Why I didn't just walk to the corner and catch the bus I'll never know.

Just as I got to the door he emerged with a six-pack of beer in his hand.

"Let's go," he said.

"I'm going back to school," I announced. "I'll catch the bus on the corner. I can probably make it back in time for my next class."

"JT, I want to be with you this afternoon. Forget that stupid school for now. Come on." He got into the car and started the motor. I turned and started down the sidewalk.

"Where you going?" Sam rolled down the window and yelled.

"I told you, I'm going back to school."

"The bus doesn't come for another forty-five minutes. You'll freeze." He didn't sound quite as drunk as before. "Come on, I'll drive you." He started to back out.

"With the way you drove on the way here, I'll never get to school alive."

"Ah, JT, I'll drive like a good little boy, I promise." He made a cross over his heart like I used to do when I was a kid. Was I ever a kid? I could hardly remember. He smiled and I couldn't help but notice that dimple in his chin. So once again I went against my better judgment. What was it about this guy? I walked around and got into the car.

"Want a beer?" Sam offered as he started down the street.

"Now what do you think? I should go back to school smelling like I just left the local tavern? No, thanks."

"Just thought I'd ask." Sam took a long swallow.

"Hey, this isn't the way to school! You didn't turn!" I frowned at him.

"I know. I never intended to take you to school. You're so naïve, JT. I thought I'd taught you better than that."

"What are you talking about? Take me to school

and *now*." I was getting angry. Who did he think he was?

"School's a drag. We're going to skip it this afternoon."

"Since when do you decide what I'm going to do?"

"Ah, come off it, JT. I always decide what we're going to do." His smile was neither amusing nor cute.

"I want you to take me to school or else let me out and I'll catch the bus."

"Oh, trying to assert yourself, huh?" Sam finished his beer and reached for another one.

"I should have known better than to come with you in the first place." I wasn't sure if I was talking more to Sam or to myself. "I'm beginning to think everyone is right. First Tom, then Renee, and everybody else that knows you and me."

"Right about what?" Sam was listening, even though I wasn't sure if he was my intended audience.

"Right about you." I turned to him and all my frustration and anger surfaced. "Ever since I met you there's been trouble. I've lost my friends. I'm in trouble at home all the time, it seems. All my great plans for doing so well in high school have disappeared. I wanted so hard to be a somebody and it seems that now I'm nothing but a nobody. And it's your fault. Just look at you."

Sam was driving faster. The speedometer was approaching fifty and we were still on a side street. "What do you mean, 'just look at me'?"

"You're nothing but a troublemaker and a boozer. You come to school drunk, you make trouble with the teachers, you laugh at the other kids. Oh, you say you care about what the kids think, but that's bull. You haven't done anything to get them to like you or accept you. You always have to be the boss, you have to be the big shot telling me what to do, how to think, how to act. Who needs this? It's that damn ladder! I should have burned it the minute I had it. Boy, you were right when you said ladder are for climbing both up and down. I've done nothing but come down ever since I met you."

Suddenly the car swerved and Sam made a U-turn right in the middle of the street. "You want to go back to school? Well, you got it, kid. Who the hell do you think you are, Miss Prissy? Just like the rest of them. You're a two-faced bitch who doesn't know up from down."

We were heading straight to school at about fifty miles an hour on the city streets. I was angry but frightened at the way Sam was driving. My mind was racing as we sped through the streets. I thought about my mother and how much I liked her. I thought about my dad, too. He really wasn't such a bad guy, if he'd just think before he talked. Tom was O.K., too. For a big brother I'd always liked him. I thought about some of the things I'd said to Sam, too. I felt kind of bad about saying them, but he wouldn't have gotten so mad unless some of it were true. I thought about Renee too and how much I missed her friendship.

Finally we reached school and the car came to a screeching halt in front of the main entrance.

Before I got out I felt a need to say something. "It could have worked out, Sam, I wish it would have. I loved you, I really did, but I can't handle this craziness. I can't stand when you're drinking. Maybe when you quit drinking and get your head on straight we can get together again." I started out the door.

"Thanks for nothing!" Sam took another swallow from the can and flipped it on the school lawn. I turned and ran up the stairs.

I was waiting for Sam to drive away, but I didn't hear the motor start. I wanted to turn around, but I was afraid to. I opened the school door and walked down the corridor. The halls were quiet so I snuck into one of the washrooms to wait until the next class started. My mind was a jumbled mess. The things I said to Sam all came tumbling back to haunt me.

I really didn't want to leave him; I really did love him. I really did want to stay with him, but not like he was. He had to do something for himself and by himself. I knew I secretly wanted him to come running after me to tell me he loved me, to tell me he wouldn't drink anymore, that he'd straighten himself out, and wouldn't I stay by his side? It was a romantic idea, but not very probable.

Just then the bell rang and kids started filling the halls. When I walked out of the bathroom I heard a long, loud bellow. It took me a couple of seconds to realize it had been my own name I'd heard and the voice was Sam's. I saw Sam coming down the hall, weaving his way through the kids. I saw him cup his hands around his mouth and call for me again. "JT!" I started toward him just as Jakness stepped out of his room and grabbed Sam by the arm. I thought I saw Jakness say something to Sam. Sam broke his arm loose and just stood staring at Jakness. I was afraid of what Jakness had said. By this time there were kids everywhere and I couldn't reach Sam and Jakness, but could see them standing right by Jakness's door. I knew Jakness was talking to Sam, but I was too far away to hear what was going on. There was a solid mass of humanity waiting to see what was going to happen, but they had left a circle of about two feet around them. I tried to push my way through the crowd, but it was hopeless. The scent of a fight had rooted the kids to the spot and they refused to move. Then the mass of kids became strangely quiet.

Sam's low voice echoed all the way to me. "Jakness, I didn't come to see you, but as long as you stopped me there are a few things I'd like to say to you, and a few things I'd like to hear you say, too."

I tried desperately to reach Sam. I started elbowing and jabbing the kids in front of me. When they turned to look, I managed to inch forward. All th time I kept thinking that if only I'd gone with S this wouldn't be happening. I just had to reach Sam and stop him from getting into trouble again.

"Sam, why don't you come in my room so we can talk about this?" Now I could see Sam's face and it was extremely pale.

"I'm not that stupid, Jakness. You want me to come in there so you can close the door and there won't be any witnesses. No, thanks."

"Sam, go into the science room and we'll talk this over." Jakness's voice was firm.

"Hey, I'm all for talking. As a matter of fact, isn't that why you stopped me—to talk to me? Or was it just to insult me some more? Yes, Jakness, I definitely think there should be some talking and it's *you* I want to hear talking. And do you know what I want to hear you talk about?" Sam was standing about a foot from Jakness. I was getting a little closer, but the going was slow.

"No, I don't."

"Well, let me tell you. I want to hear you apologizing to me in front of all these nice kids who have gathered on this momentous occasion."

"Apologize for what?" I could see Jakness getting angry, but he kept his voice controlled.

"For calling me an ignorant dope pusher, and this time I want you to mean it. That apology of yours was as phony as the oregano some of the kids sell around here as marijuana."

"I don't know what you're talking about."

"Oh, yes you do, Jakness. You know exactly what I'm talking about."

"My apology was a sincere one."

"Bullshit!" Sam's voice exploded from him. "The only reason you apologized was to save your own neck."

Just then we heard an authoritarian voice coming through the swarm of kids. "Move back. Stand aside. What's going on here?"

"Oh, no," I heard myself groaning aloud. It was

Wilson. Of all the teachers to get here first, why did it have to be him? When everyone turned, it gave me the chance to move closer.

I managed to reach Sam just in time to hear Jakness hiss to Sam, "You're dead now, you stupid son of a bitch!"

Since everyone else was parting the waters for Wilson, I figured Sam and I were the only ones to hear the remark. When Sam turned, Jakness grabbed his arm and tried to shove him into the science room.

"Don't touch me, you phony bastard!" Sam's fist shot out and he clipped Jakness in the jaw as he tried to free himself from Jakness's grip. Jakness stumbled backward, and Sam was on him instantly. By this time, Wilson had reached the circle.

"Bensen, I should have known. You're finished now. Absolutely one hundred percent finished." When he started for Sam, I jumped in front of him to block his way.

Just then Sam leaped off Jakness, and Jakness pulled himself up. "Leave him alone," I screamed.

"Who are you?" Wilson moved a little closer, but my interference took him by surprise and he faltered.

"I'm his friend." I nodded toward Sam and saw the old familiar smile fleet across his face for just an instant.

"That's right, she sure is," Sam added.

"You have pretty bad taste, that's for sure. Now get out of the way." Jakness too moved closer.

"Mr. Jakness, please, this won't solve anything."

"Get out of the way, Jeannie. Bensen is through. He'll never walk these halls again." Jakness's voice was shaking.

"He may never walk again period," Wilson added.

Just then I saw a flash of metal. I turned to see Sam spring open a switchblade. "Sam, don't," I pleaded with my voice and eyes.

"I have no choice now, JT. You heard what th said." He seemed so calm about it all. "Move o the way, so you don't get hurt. Call my dad when it's all over. He'll know what to do."

"Somebody stop them, *please!*" I turned to the crowd for help. But everyone just stood there waiting for the sight of blood. I couldn't believe what was happening. At that moment, Jakness pushed me to the side and rushed for Sam. At the same time, Wilson went for Sam, too.

I fell into two kids and regained my balance just in time to see Sam's foot hit Wilson in the stomach. Jakness grabbed Sam's arm as Sam swung with the knife. Jakness jumped back and the knife screamed in the air. Suddenly Wilson started yelling.

"Help me, help me!" His arms crossed and he was grasping his chest. "My heart, help!" There was mass confusion then. He fell to the floor moaning. Jakness stopped his assault on Sam. Just then the crowd parted for the principal and another teacher. As the three immediately bent to help Wilson, it was all the edge Sam needed. Before even I was aware what was happening, Sam disappeared in the crowd.

"Call an ambulance!" the principal's voice barked. "What happened here?" He turned to Jakness, who was unbuttoning Wilson's shirt and removing his tie.

"It's Bensen here, causing real trouble this time." He turned to the spot where Sam had been. Everyone else turned too and then we all knew.

"Where's Bensen?" Jakness was on his feet screaming. "Where's Bensen? Where did that son of a bitch go?"

"Jakness, take it easy." The principal was on his feet grabbing Jakness by the arm. "Watch what you're saying. We have enough trouble already." The tone of his voice was definitely a command, but Jakness either didn't hear him, or chose not to.

"I'll get him. If it's the last thing I do, I'll get that little bastard. No punk kid makes a fool of me and gets away with it. He tried once before, but never again!"

"Jakness, shut up!" This time the principal grabbed his arm and shook him. "That's enough."

Just then the other teacher returned. "The ambulance is on its way." He was flanked by the school nurse.

"Everyone to their classes. Come on, let's go." The principal made one quiet, simple request and the crowd started breaking up. In a daze, I turned and hurried to the front of the building. Sam's car was nowhere in sight.

Chapter 16

Fighting back tears, I went to gym class because I didn't know what else to do. I knew I should have been angry with Sam, but I just wasn't. At least he knew I still cared about him. I felt so guilty because Sam was only in school to see me. Why hadn't I just gone with him? None of this would have happened. I kept seeing that knife in Sam's hand. Why had he done that? Now I was sure charges would be brought against him. He didn't have a chance, and Wilson, God, the guy must have had a heart attack or something. I wondered if he were still alive.

As we walked to the locker room one of the girls asked, "Do you really go out with Sam Bensen?"

"Yeah, you could say that."

"Well, he's some tough guy. I've never been around a scene like that before."

"Oh."

"You weren't bad yourself. I heard Jakness started it all, is that true?"

"Where did you hear that?" I couldn't believe Sam wasn't being blamed again for all the trouble.

"Oh, one of my friends was at his locker when Sam first came in, and he told me Jakness grabbed Sam as he was going down the hall and called him 'a sneaky dope-pushing son of a bitch who would regret doing imitations of him in the parking lot!'"

"So that's what started it all," I said more to myself than to the girl. I knew Jakness had said something to Sam and now I knew why Sam had gotten so mad.

"Jakness made a real fool out of himself at the d, didn't he?"

"Yeah," I mumbled.

"Too bad Sam had that knife. That'll do him in, I'm afraid."

"I know."

"Say, what's Sam really like?" The question surprised me. Since then it has been asked many times. I didn't have an answer then; I don't have an answer now.

"That's kind of hard to say." I paused for a long time.

"Well, good luck to both of you." She turned and walked off.

When she left I didn't know where I was going, but I needed to find Sam. I had this terrible feeling in the back of my throat. The feeling always scared me. It was the same feeling I had when I knew my grandmother was dying and when I found out in third grade my best friend was moving to Boston. I hoped this feeling was only my own fear and not because of impending disaster.

I left the school building and found a pay phone. Nobody answered at Sam's house. I let it ring at least thirty times just in case Sam walked in, or his dad was sleeping. Sam had said something about calling his dad when it was all over, so they must have been on speaking terms again. When nobody answered, I started walking, hoping Sam would pick me up. No such luck though. Finally, I just gave up and went home.

I tried reading the paper, but even Ann Landers couldn't cheer me up. I put the paper down and decided to fix supper. Maybe I could talk to Mom tonight. Maybe she could give me some insight into all this craziness. Meanwhile, I kept watching for Sam's car to drive by, but it never did.

The phone brought me out of my daydreams. "Hello," I said, my heart pounding. Would it be Sam?

"Hi, it's me." My throat tightened and my heart sank.

"Hi, Tom, what's up?"

"Tell Mom and Dad I won't be home for supper. I'm working late tonight."

"O.K., nobody's home yet." I paused and Tom must have sensed something.

"Are you all right, Jeannie? I heard what happened today." His voice almost sounded understanding.

"Yeah, I figure everybody has by now." My depression came through loud and clear.

"Everything is going to work out, don't worry."

"How can I help but worry? I know you hate Sam, but he is my friend and I care about him." All my frustrations were coming out. I realized I really needed someone to talk to.

"Jeannie, I don't hate Sam. Maybe I was wrong about him. Knowing Jakness I should have figured it wasn't all Sam's fault. I'm sorry I yelled at you the other night, too."

"That's O.K., Tom. Let's just forget it. Have you heard anything about Wilson?" Even though I didn't like the guy, I hoped he'd be all right.

"Well, I heard he's in pretty bad shape, Jeannie. But maybe that was just a rumor."

"Yeah, maybe. Well, see you later."

"O.K., hang in there little sister. Bye."

Now I really felt terrible. What if Wilson died? Would Sam be held responsible? Where was he anyway?

Just then I heard Dad come into the house. I was glad not to be alone. "Hi, Dad." I tried to smile when I saw the scowl on his face.

"Oh, hello." He walked past me as if I didn't even exist.

I followed him into the kitchen. "Are you O.K., Dad?"

"No, damn it, I'm not," he yelled as he slammed his fist on the table. I jumped back. "But it's no ncern of yours." He must have sensed my fright because he got up and patted my shoulder on his way to the living room. He picked up the paper and slumped down into his chair. I decided the best approach was to stay away. I wondered where Mom was. I kept looking at the chicken and realized supper would be done soon. Finally I stood in the door.

"Supper is about ready. Do you know when Mom will be home?"

Dad slammed the paper down and shouted, "How the hell should I know? I went down there to get her and she wasn't in the office. So I decided to wait for her in the bar down the street. I walk in and who do I see sitting at the bar but your mother—and she wasn't alone. Get it? Not alone. Here I work my ass off and she's hotfooting around with some other guy. Why are you asking me if she's home? Why not ask her new friend?"

I was stunned. I couldn't believe what my father was saying. My mother would never do anything like that. Dad had to be wrong.

"I'm sure there was a good reason, Dad. Did you talk to her?"

"Are you crazy? Two's company, three's a crowd, if you know what I mean."

"Dad, you're wrong about Mom, I know you are." I should have known better than trying to defend Mom, but at that time I wasn't smart enough to know when to stay out of my parents' fights.

"Stop defending her. You'd stick up for her no matter what she did." Dad was standing by the window. He stood for a long time with his hands in his pockets. His sagging shoulders made me realize how defeated he must feel.

"Dad, Mom loves you, I know she does." This conversation was a nightmare. I was crying and my words were barely audible.

Dad turned from the window. All the anger was gone from his face. He slowly walked over to me "Jeannie, I'm sorry. I should never have told yo'

He walked into the hallway and slowly climbed the stairs. I had never in my life felt so miserable. My whole world was collapsing around me and there was nothing I could do. First my friends, then Sam, and now my family.

At seven thirty I couldn't stand the tension anymore. I knocked on Dad's door, told him I was sick and said I was going to bed. Immediately I climbed down the ladder. Dad was in such a state I was sure he hadn't heard me leave. I was so glad to be out of the house because I not only wanted to find Sam, I sure didn't want to be home when my mom arrived. I figured that was one scene I could do without. I wandered down the street. I don't know what I hoped to see or find out, but I was worried sick about Sam. I called his house again. After a couple of rings, I heard his father's voice.

"Hello."

"Hello, Mr. Bensen, this is Jeannie Tanger, JT. I was wondering if Sam was around?"

"Oh, hello, you're Sam's girlfriend, aren't you?"

"Yes, I am." He sounded sober.

"Well, it seems you, me, and the police are all wondering where Sam is."

"The police?" Instantly my heart started beating faster and my breath became shorter. "What do the police want?"

"Jakness is pressing charges against Sam for assault and battery. The knife Sam had makes it pretty serious, I guess. What a mess!" Mr. Bensen sighed. I felt so bad about this whole dilemma I just wanted to sit down and cry.

"Say, JT, were you there when all this happened today?"

"Yeah, I was there."

"Maybe you can tell me what happened? I've been wondering if the version I heard from the police is one-sided."

"Sure, I can tell you what I saw." I proceeded to tell him my story.

When I finished he said, "Well, the police were pretty darn accurate. I was hoping it wasn't that bad, but I guess it was. Poor Sam. He's had such a rough life and now it only seems to be getting worse for him. If only his mother had stayed around. Maybe things would have been different."

I didn't want to hear this. I didn't think I was the one to console Mr. Bensen. "Well, if you hear from Sam let me know, will you?" I knew I was being rude, but I couldn't stand it. First Dad and now Mr. Bensen. All I wanted to do was find Sam, not listen to everybody else's problems.

I went back outside not knowing what I was doing or where I was going when Jeb unexpectedly pulled up. The wind was blowing so I was glad to get out of the cold. But he didn't look too happy as I opened the door.

"Hi."

"Hi, have you heard the news?" Jeb asked.

"What news?" For some inexplicable reason I felt afraid.

"Wilson died a little while ago. I guess his heart just couldn't take the excitement."

"Oh, no." My thought turned to Sam. "Now what, Jeb?"

"I don't know. I'm really worried about Sam."

"Have you seen him?"

"Not since I helped him get out of school."

"Oh, so you're the one who helped him. I wondered how he'd disappeared so quickly. Thanks for doing that, Jeb."

"You know, you're not the only friend Sam has. I care about him, too." Jeb's voice was both angry and sad.

"I'm sorry, I know you are. It's just sometimes I forget. You know what I mean." I looked to Jeb for both forgiveness and understanding. Right now needed somebody. I didn't want to be out on the street alone. If only I could feel Sam's arms around me.

"Just forget it. It's no big deal. I just wish I'd gotten there earlier. I might have been able to get him away from Jakness before he pulled that knife." We drove in silence for a while. "I'm afraid Sam is going to be in big trouble now. Crazy Jakness is more than likely out looking for Sam." Jeb broke the silence with the same thoughts I'd been having.

"Do you have any idea where Sam might be?" I quizzed Jeb.

"Maybe he's at home."

"No, I just talked to his dad and he's not at home."

"Well, let's just hope he isn't sitting somewhere in his car getting drunk." Jeb had voiced my silent fear.

"Hey, maybe I do know where he is." I'd just thought of that place behind the grove of trees I had gone to with Sam the night we had sat and talked for so long. "Jeb, I have an idea. I'm not sure exactly where this place is, but I can try to find it. Are you game?"

"Sure, what do we have to lose?"

I told Jeb what I could remember and we decided to try to find the spot. First Jeb wanted to stop at Arly's, the local hangout.

"Maybe somebody will know something here. I see a couple of guys I want to talk to a second. Want to come?" Jeb said after we pulled in.

"No, thanks, I'll wait here for you." When Jeb left I started thinking about what might be going on at home. I couldn't believe Dad's accusations about Mom. She wouldn't do something like that. She just couldn't. I had enough problems of my own; I wasn't about to admit how serious my parents' problems were, too. I just couldn't deal with anything else right now. Just then Jeb returned to the car. He got in and we started down the street.

"So what did you find out?"

"The police are looking everywhere for Sam," Jeb finally answered. "Things are really serious now."

"What do you mean?" I was panicking.

"That damn Jakness is pressing charges against Sam and now he is pushing for murder since Wilson died."

"But his death isn't Sam's fault." I couldn't believe what Jeb had said.

"You and I know that, but I wonder what Sam is thinking. I sure as hell hope he isn't feeling responsible. Of course he might not even know."

"What a mess!" I wanted this nightmare to end.

"Now tell me again where you think this place you and Sam went might be. We have to find him."

"Did you hear anything else?" Somehow I had the feeling he was holding back.

"Yeah, Jakness is out looking for Sam, too. God help us if that maniac finds him first."

"God help Sam, you mean." Jeb didn't answer. What could he say anyway?

Chapter 17

Sure enough, behind the grove of trees was the green bug. The motor was running and for an instant I had visions of finding Sam dead on the seat of the car from carbon monoxide poisoning. But as soon as we pulled up beside the car, Sam turned his head and I knew he was alive.

I went around to the passenger side and opened the door.

"Sam! Jeb and I have been looking for you."

"So, now you've found me." He didn't sound drunk, thank God.

"We've been worried." Sam didn't answer.

"Hey, buddy, can we get in the car? It's freezing out here."

"Go ahead." Jeb crawled into the back seat and I got in the front.

"That was some daring escape we pulled off, wasn't it?" Jeb seemed determined to keep the tone light. At that moment, I loved Jeb for trying so hard. I also realized how much he cared for Sam.

"Hey, thanks for that." Sam turned to Jeb. For just a second the frown left his face. "That was just like a miracle. I can't believe I got out of there. I was so scared."

"Well, you sure played it cool. You looked perfectly calm and in complete control," Jeb assured him.

"You should have seen the look on Jakness's face when he realized you were gone," I added.

"Yeah." Sam looked at me and for a moment I saw a brown sparkle. "Well, thanks to my buddy here,

I didn't have the pleasure of seeing Jakness taken by surprise."

"By the time I got back, the principal had dispersed everyone, so I didn't get to see Jakness either," Jeb said.

We all lapsed into silence, remembering the horrible afternoon. Finally Sam broke the quiet. "How's Wilson doing? Anybody hear anything?" Sam was staring out the window and his questions weren't really directed at either of us. I chose not to answer and Jeb finally did.

"Well, Sam, that's sort of the reason we've been looking for you."

"I suppose the police are after me, too, because of that damn knife. I'm sure there must be a law against weapons in school. If there isn't, I'm sure Wilson will dig one up."

"Wilson isn't going to be digging much of anything anymore," Jeb added.

"What do you mean?"

"Sam, Wilson had a heart attack, and died a couple of hours ago." I reached for Sam's hand when I told him.

"There's more bad news, Sam. Jakness is pressing charges against you," Jeb said.

"Figures. What are the charges?"

"Well, they were assault and battery." Jeb paused and then continued. "But now he's trying to charge you with murder. He's going to try to stick Wilson's death on you."

"That son of a bitch! Well, I'll just have to find him and set him straight." Sam's voice was stony cold.

"That won't be hard. We were at Arly's and I heard Jakness is out looking for you," Jeb added.

"Sam, fighting with Jakness is no way to settle anything. Let's just go to the police and you can turn yourself in and all of this will be taken care of the right way," I blurted out. "Jeb and I will go wit' you, too. Won't we, Jeb?" I turned to Jeb and gave him my most pleading look.

"Sure, if that's what Sam wants to do."

"Turn myself in? JT, sometimes your naïveté amazes me. What do you think is going to happen to me if I turn myself in?"

"Nothing, in comparison to what will happen if you go after Jakness."

"JT, Jakness and I have a score to settle. When that's settled, I'm taking off."

"Sam, that's crazy. You go after Jakness and you'll never have a prayer with the police, and if you run, they'll find you." Sam's set jaw told me my pleading was falling on deaf ears.

Jeb interrupted my thoughts. "Hey, old buddy, where would you go? And with what?" If Jeb had accepted the fact that Sam was going after Jakness, I hadn't.

"I've got a plan. Now it'll just be a little delayed because of that jerk Jakness."

"What kind of plan? What are you going to do?" I asked.

"I'm going to San Diego to find my mother."

"What?" I was shocked. "San Diego! Do you think you're going to make it all the way to California with the police looking for you?" I tried to remain calm.

"Yeah, I think I'll be able to sneak by them."

"How?"

"First I'm going to hide this little green bug," Sam patted the dashboard, "and then I'm going to take a bus to Minneapolis. From there I'm going to catch a train to the West Coast."

"What makes you think the police won't be watching the bus and train stations?" I knew Sam thought the police were stupid, but I was beginning to think Sam was the crazy one.

"That, my dear sweetheart, is where you come in."

"What do you mean—me?" I wasn't about to let ʌt word "sweetheart" be my undoing.

"You're going to tell the police that I took off in my car for New York."

"New York? Are you crazy?"

"No, I have an uncle there. So if the police ask my dad if there is any reason I might go to New York, he'll say yes."

"You mean you're going to take off without telling your dad?" I couldn't believe this.

"Yeah, I've got to. My old man might tell the police if he knows. I can't take that chance. I'll call him when I get to California."

"But, Sam," I started.

"No buts, JT. This is the only way. All you and Jeb have to do is tell the police I was talking about New York. I have been, too, so it's not a lie."

"Are you sure, Sam?" Jeb pressed.

"I'm sure, Jeb. There's nothing else I can do. As soon as I find Jakness and settle a score with him, I'll be on my way."

"If that's what you want, Sam," Jeb answered.

"It's the only way and it'll work, too, if you two do your part." Sam looked at me and squeezed my hand. "I know I can count on both of you."

"No sweat, Sam. You can count on me," Jeb said.

"Thanks, Jeb. I owe you and someday I'll repay you." Sam reached over the seat and extended his hand to Jeb. As they shook hands, I saw the deep friendship and love that was in their eyes, their touch, and their smiles.

Sam let go of Jeb's hand and turned to me.

Before he could say anything Jeb said, "Hey, I think I'll wait in my car."

I opened the door and Jeb crawled out. As he walked away he squeezed my hand. "Hang in there, JT. It's all going to work out."

I hated Sam's plan, but I didn't know how I'd get him to change his mind. Before I could even try, Sam put his arm around my shoulder and pulled me close to him.

"Oh, Sam, what's happening to us?" Sam's touch and the feel of his breathing on my face as I leaned against his shoulder was my undoing. I could feel the tears I had fought so hard to keep repressed these last few hours beginning to surface. I could feel my throat tighten and I struggled to keep from sobbing. Sam pulled me even closer and buried his face in my hair. After a long silence, Sam answered.

"I don't know, JT. Everything has become a nightmare. I feel so helpless and out of control. I feel like my brain cells are one by one being crushed and I'm slowly losing the ability to think and figure things out. I just want this all to end."

"It will, Sam. I don't know how or when, but it will end." I wanted Sam to comfort me, but I knew Sam needed my comforting and love more. All my being reached out to him.

"JT, do you know what I wish more than anything?"

"What, Sam?"

"I wish we were back in that science class when I first saw you. I wish we were starting over. I would do so many things differently. Remember that day, JT?"

"Sure, how could I forget it?"

"I remember how depressed I was when I walked into that class. Then I saw you and I thought, hey, maybe things weren't going to be so bad after all. I remember I glanced at your books and I saw your initials on your notebook. Then I decided to say hello."

"Yeah, I didn't realize you were talking to me. I couldn't think of anything to say. I felt like I was swimming in those gorgeous eyes of yours."

"I loved your soft voice. I forgot what you told me your name was, so all hour I sat there trying to figure out what JT stood for. I finally decided it must mean you were 'Just Terrific' and all hour I kept thinking of Just Terrific and how much fun we could have."

"All I could think about was how well your jeans fit." We both laughed.

"So when science class ended I said 'See you, JT' for my 'Just Terrific' new girl."

"You mean you decided right then and there I'd be your girl?"

"Sure. You don't think I listened to Jakness that whole hour, do you? Some of my best daydreams about us were in that classroom with you beside me. So many times I just wanted to grab you and run out of the room."

"You're crazy, Sam, you know that?"

"I think you've said that one or two times before." Sam bent his head just enough so he was about two inches from my face. For a long time, Sam just looked at me. "I don't ever want to forget what you look like, JT. I love you." His lips met mine with a fierceness neither one of us had ever known. Each of us wanted to become the other. The mingling of our lips was like the mingling of our hearts. At that moment the desire to become one was overpowering and I lost all thought. I felt our bodies crushing against one another and the fear I had of losing Sam became overwhelming.

When at last our bodies parted, silent tears flowed down my face. They were mixed with Sam's as I saw him fight for control of the raw emotion that had been ripped from both of us. I gently wiped his tears and kissed his eyes. Our sharing of true feelings had never been deeper.

When the tears had dried and I could trust my voice I spoke. "Sam, I'm going to help you, under one condition. If you don't agree, I'm not going to lie for you."

"Is this blackmail?" Sam laughed.

"Call it what you like, but I'm very serious, Sam."

"Well, tell me. You have my complete attention." Sam pulled back and waited.

"I'll only help you if you leave now and forget about finding Jakness."

"What?" Sam was incredulous.

"I mean it, Sam. There's been enough trouble. I want you to leave immediately and forget revenge."

"But I owe that son of a bitch! He's trying to put a murder rap on me." Sam's fingers were drumming the seat.

"I know that, but it won't stick. If you just let everything cool off, that charge will be dropped and then we can worry about the others."

"You're serious, aren't you?" Sam's head was slightly tilted. I knew that thoughtful look.

"I'm deadly serious. Either you leave now or I'm going to call your dad and tell him everything."

Suddenly Sam was laughing. "JT, you're great. I've seen you change from a shy, scared juvenile into a cool, calculating woman and I love it. I suppose if I have to, I agree."

"Oh, Sam, I knew you would." I threw my arms around his neck and gave him a good old smooch.

"Come on, let's see what Jeb is up to. He's probably fallen asleep by now." Sam started to get out of the car, but I grabbed his shoulder.

"Sam, maybe I should go with you?"

Sam looked at me and I saw tears in his eyes. "Oh, JT, I've thought of that a hundred times today, but I don't think it's best."

"Why not?" I wasn't sure I wanted to go, but the thought of losing Sam was tearing me apart.

"If something happened, what would we do? Besides, I don't have enough money for both of us."

"I just don't want to lose you." I clung to him in desperation.

"I'll be back. When all of this blows over, I'll come back. I promise."

"Sam, will you call me when you can?" My stomach felt hollow.

"Of course I will. Don't worry, sweetheart, we aren't ended yet. In fact, we've only just started."

"I'm going to hold you to your promise, Sam." But for some unexplainable reason I didn't feel at all good about that promise. In fact, I felt a cold fear in the back of my throat, but I decided to push my terrible thoughts as far back in my brain as I could.

Jeb's car was nice and warm. I got in and Sam slid in beside me.

"Hey, Jeb, thought you fell asleep there for a while."

"Yeah, I almost did. So is everything all set?" Jeb looked at Sam.

"I think so, but it seems, old buddy, the plan has been slightly altered due to some convincing pressure by this young woman here." Sam looked at me, laughed, and shook his head.

"Oh, yeah, what's the change?" Jeb pushed himself up on the seat and waited for us to explain.

"JT has coerced me into agreeing not to go back into the city to find Jakness. I'm going to take off for California right away."

Jeb gave Sam the strangest look. "Really?"

"Really," Sam said, "so let's go over the plan once again."

I still wasn't too hot about Sam's running away, but at least I'd gotten him to give up that crazy idea of evening the score with Jakness. Now I'd have to do my best to convince everyone that Sam had gone to New York.

At last we had worked out every detail. We lingered in the car for a few awkward moments. Nobody wanted to make the final move. Finally I couldn't take it anymore. "Sam, I think it's time to go." My voice was barely a whisper. My eyes darted everywhere except at Sam.

"Yeah, I know." Sam reached over and extended his hand to Jeb for the second time that night.

"Thanks for everything, old buddy. Hope I can repay you someday."

"You're welcome, Sam. Good luck. Next time we're together we'll bend our elbows a few times and toast all the morons in this stupid town."

"Yeah." Sam laughed and punched Jeb in the shoulder.

I sat immobilized. I wanted this moment of good-bye to end and yet I wanted to be able to see Sam forever. Already I was memorizing every line of his face. I wanted to burn into my memory that smile, that soft dimple, and those gorgeous eyes. I felt a tear sneak out of my left eye. I tried to brush it away, but Sam softly wiped it for me. His hand tilted my chin and his lips lightly brushed mine.

"Hang in there, sweetheart. Things might get tough, but you'll be just fine. Remember our ladder!"

He was out of the car before I could even form a response. All those profound things I had wanted to say were left suspended in my mind. My body felt like it was being dragged, screaming and kicking, behind the car and yet I hadn't moved a muscle. Only my tear ducts were working and they were screaming in a silent, yet violent way.

As Jeb drove back to town, we were both lost in our own thoughts. I couldn't believe Sam was really gone. When would I see him again? All of this seemed so absurd. How one argument in school led to anger and violence and even death seemed so senseless. For just a flash, I had a glimpse of how sad and wrong life could be. I felt I was finally growing up and I didn't like it at all. I wanted to hide in the cocoon of the sandbox and the backyard swing set. No more real life for me, please. I'm only a kid, leave me be.

Chapter 18

We pulled into Arly's because Jeb wanted to be sure lots of people saw us. Neither of us realized it was past midnight and most kids were home.

All I could think about was how convincingly I would lie when the police asked me about Sam. Oh, how I hoped they wouldn't come to the house. Dad would just go crazy if the police came to his sacred abode to interrogate his daughter. Considering everything else that had happened lately, this would probably put him over the edge.

I was getting cold. The temperature had dropped and the sky was overcast. Snowflakes were just beginning to fall and the wind was blowing.

Soon a couple of Jeb's buddies came over to the car and slipped into the back seat. I knew them from Jeb's parties. One was Terry and the other was Steve.

"Hey, Jeb, what's happening?" Terry inquired.

"Not much. Has Jakness been around?" Jeb got right to the point.

"Yeah, he was here an hour or so ago," Steve piped up. "He'd been to at least one of the local bars, and was feeling no pain."

"Have you seen Bensen?" Terry wanted to know.

"Yeah," Jeb answered. "He's heading for New York until things cool off, but don't say anything if the police ask, O.K.?" The plan was beginning to take shape.

"No, we won't say anything. Hope he makes it," Steve said.

"Good idea for him to get out of here," Terry added. "That crazy Jakness should be put in jail. Hope he cools off before something bad happens."

"Did you hear what Jakness wants to do?"

"No, but I can guess." Jeb's remarks made me nervous. I wasn't sure I wanted to know what Jakness was up to.

"He's spreading the word that he wants to challenge Sam to a game of chicken—winner take all—one survivor."

Jeb shook his head. "He's crazy, that man is a certified loony. God, I hope Sam doesn't come back to the city."

"What do you mean—winner take all—one survivor?" My mind was in a daze, yet I knew that chicken was a very serious game.

Steve took a long look at me, then said, "It means you play until someone is too hurt to drive."

For a second my heart stopped and then I remembered. Sam was on his way to California; he wasn't coming back to the city.

When I looked up, Brian and Renee were pulling into the parking lot. What were they doing at Arly's? Brian got out of his car and ran over to another one. He talked to them briefly and did the same at another car. Then he began walking quickly in our direction. When he knocked on the car window, I rolled it down. The last people I'd expected to see were Renee and Brian, but so far this whole day had been one unexpected event after another. Why should it change now?

"Jeannie, we've been looking all over for you," Brian said. "Your parents are frantic. The police are looking for you. I guess they're at your house."

"So why are *you* looking for me?" Somehow I still couldn't make the connection.

"Your parents called Renee. They thought maybe she'd know where you were."

"They sure don't know anything about me, do they, if they thought Renee would know where I was." My sarcasm came through loud and clear.

Renee had come up behind Brian in time to catch

that last snide remark. "Hey, Jeannie, cool the insults. Your parents are really worried. And so was I." The last statement was barely audible, but I knew I'd heard correctly. I didn't respond even though I wanted to.

Brian broke the silence. "Why don't you let us take you home?"

"I can take you home, if you want to go." Jeb came to my immediate rescue.

I looked at my watch and then at Jeb. By now Sam should have had plenty of time to be well on his way to catching the morning bus. This had been a long day and night. I was ready to go home, crawl under the warm quilt and go to sleep. If Mom was home, maybe there would be someone to save me from the ravings of my father. If I could just block everything out, maybe things would look better in the morning.

"Come on, Jeannie. I'll go home with you." Renee must have sensed my near exhaustion and dread of facing home.

"O.K." I couldn't hassle anymore. "Thanks, Jeb. See you fellows." I turned to the guys in back and gave a slight wave. On the way to Brian's car, I noticed the snow was coming down in large flakes and sticking to the ground. Soon everything would be covered. I remember thinking the snow would certainly favor Sam's getaway.

"Your mom and dad have been frantic looking for you," Renee said on the way home.

"Who called you?" I was worried about how things had been when Mom got home. Boy, that conversation with Dad sure seemed a long time ago.

"Your mom did. She seemed practically hysterical." When I didn't respond, Renee continued. "They thought you ran away with Sam."

"Why did they think that?" How had Sam entered the picture?

"Your mom said something about a rope ladder out your window."

"Oh, no." How I wished I'd figured out a way to lower it from the window once I'd come down.

"Jeannie, have you really been using a ladder to sneak out of your house?" It was hard to tell from Renee's voice if it was sarcasm or admiration. I was too tired to figure it out and too tired to care either way.

"Yeah." Why deny what was the obvious truth?

"Was that Bensen's idea?" Brian asked.

"What difference does it make whose idea it was?" I leaned my head against the seat and felt my aching back muscles.

"I was just curious, that's all." My answer quieted him temporarily.

"Did you talk to my dad at all?"

"No, just your mother. I could hear your dad in the background."

"I suppose he was yelling?" I asked.

"Yeah, I'm afraid he was," Renee answered.

Renee seemed pretty sympathetic tonight. Or maybe I was just too tired and was missing the subtleties in her voice. Renee continued, "The police were at your house, too. I guess they were looking for Sam."

"I'm not surprised." I started going over in my mind exactly what I would say to the police. I hoped I would be a convincing liar. Better still, maybe they'd be gone when I got there.

"Where is Sam, anyway?" Leave it to Brian to get right to the point. At least I'd have the opportunity to test out my lying skills.

"He's on his way to New York," I answered.

"How come you didn't go with him?" If only they knew how we had considered it.

"Did you think I did?" I asked Renee.

"Yeah, sort of, considering how serious you two seemed," Renee answered.

"Yeah, we were." At that moment I realized how important Sam was to me. I loved him, but I also knew I couldn't give up my whole life for him. I realized I was still my own person and that I would make it. I knew the next few months and the next few days in particular would be tough, but I'd be O.K. When Sam came back, we'd start again.

After a while, Renee turned to me. "I guess you were right about Jakness all along. That guy has proved to be a real maniac."

"It wasn't me that was right. It was Sam who spotted Jakness for what he was a long time ago."

"Did you hear he's trying to pin Wilson's death on Sam?" Brian always had good news.

"Yeah, we heard."

"Everybody knows that's a farce, but it does mean the police will have to pick up Sam and go through the formalities." Did Renee sound like she was on Sam's side?

"Sam is still wanted though for having a weapon in school. He'll be charged with assault and battery," Brian added.

"Yeah, but I think he can be tried as a juvenile and he'll probably just get probation considering the circumstances." I wondered if Sam would ever be able to walk up to my front door and take me on a real date.

"That's right. If someone under eighteen is up for murder he or she is tried as an adult," Brian went on.

"Well, the murder rap will be dropped, I'm sure," Renee cut in.

Just then we pulled up to my street. As we turned the corner we slid a little. "Boy, it sure is getting icy on the roads."

A police car was in front of our house. "Oh, I hoped they'd be gone," I moaned. All I wanted to do was crawl under my nice warm covers and go to sleep. I wasn't sure if I was coherent enough to lie well.

As I got out of the car, I wondered what the scene inside would be like, but I was too tired and miserable to really care.

When I opened the front door, I felt the warm air on my face and smelled the coffee. I saw my mother first. She was off the couch and coming toward me as soon as I stepped in. She looked frazzled. For the first time ever it occurred to me my mother was getting old. Her hair was a mess and she had little lines around her eyes. She had obviously been crying. She paused when she got to me. She seemed hesitant, almost like she was afraid.

"Hi, Mom," I whispered and then I was in her arms. I could feel her arms encircle me and I could feel her soft skin against my face. It was good to be home.

I felt something wet on my cheek and drew back. Mom was weeping silently. "Oh, Mom." I gave her the reassuring hug this time.

"We've been so worried, Jeannie. We're so glad you're home." At that moment, I loved my mom. No yelling, no accusations, no threats, just good old-fashioned reassurances that I was loved and welcomed. Just then I saw my father come up beside me. Oh, boy, I thought, here comes trouble.

"We're both glad you're home, as Mom said." My dad's voice was low and sincere. I couldn't believe it. Was this the man who earlier this evening (it *was* earlier this evening, wasn't it, and not weeks ago like it seemed?) was ranting and raving like a madman? His kindness was too much. I untangled myself from my mother and found myself being smothered in my father's huge arms. It had been so long since he had hugged me.

"Jeannie, I love you. I'm so sorry if I upset you earlier. It's all my fault you took off." Dad was talking fast.

I looked up at my dad. He looked like he'd been

crying, too. "Dad, my leaving had nothing to do with you. I just had to see Sam, that's all."

"Speaking of Sam, where is the Bensen boy?" The policemen had kept discreetly back, but now they were anxious to get on with their night's work. An older man whose name tag said O'Malley had spoken.

"I'm not exactly sure," I said falteringly.

"Where do you think he might be?" O'Malley asked.

"I'd rather not say if I don't have to." I tried to look young and defenseless.

"I'm afraid you do have to, young lady. Getting yourself into trouble by not cooperating with the police isn't going to do you or him any good at all." O'Malley was insistent, but his voice was kind.

I paused long enough for them to figure I was thinking everything over and then I said, "I think he may be on his way to New York."

"New York? Why would he go there?" the policeman asked.

"He's probably afraid of what Jakness wants to do." I swung around as Renee spoke. "Mr. Jakness is the one who should be picked up, not Sam."

"What do you mean, young lady?" The other policeman took a step forward. His name tag read Pearsly.

"Well, everybody knows Jakness has been all over town making threats against Sam. If you were in Sam's place wouldn't you take off, too?" I just wanted to hug Renee. Maybe I still did have one friend.

Just then a call came through on Pearsly's walkie-talkie. I heard the name Bensen on the radio. The policeman asked, "Are you sure it's Bensen? His girlfriend just said he's on his way to New York." There was an answer that wasn't audible to me, but the policeman continued, "O.K., we'll be right there." He put the walkie-talkie back on his belt and looked straight at me. "I thought you said your boyfriend was on his way to New York?"

"I thought he was!" Had something gone wrong already? Nobody could have spotted him yet. I could feel my heart starting to pound fast.

"Well, he has obviously changed his mind. He was at Arly's a little while ago."

"Come on, Hank, let's go see what we can do." They started for the door.

"I'm going, too!" Why had Sam come back to the city? I just had to find out what was happening. Then I remembered Jakness's challenge. Was that it?

"Honey, it's late," Mom cut in. "There isn't anything you can do now. Sam will be fine."

"No, I'm going!"

Brian and Renee were still standing by the door. My mother looked confused and tired.

"Jeannie, do you really think you have to go? It's late and it's been a long day." She paused and then said, "Your father and I would like to talk to you, too."

"Mom, I have to see if Sam's all right. I just have to." I put all the emphasis I could on the last words.

"O.K." Mom sighed and turned to Renee and Brian and said, "I think you two should go home. It's late and your parents will be concerned. Thanks for finding Jeannie."

"That's O.K.," Renee answered. She turned to me and said, "Jeannie, call me tomorrow, O.K.?"

"Sure." I was surprised she wanted me to call. Something had definitely changed Renee's attitude tonight.

"Don't forget," she added.

"I won't." I turned to Brian. "Thanks for bringing me home," I said.

Chapter 19

As soon as they left, I put my coat on. "If you're too tired, maybe Tom could drive me?" I suggested when I looked at Dad. He looked awful.

"He's not home. He's out looking for you," Mom said.

"Oh." What could I say? The whole family was involved.

"Come on, Jeannie, if it means that much to you, we'll take you. We'll leave a note for Tom," Dad said.

Outside the wind had picked up and the snow was swirling around. The sidewalks were slippery and I pulled my scarf tight around my neck to keep the chill out.

"The car will warm up fast, honey," Dad assured me as he pulled out of the driveway. "Where to?"

"Turn north, I want to go to Arly's," I answered as my tired body sank into the cushions of the back seat.

When we were on the road, Mom turned to me. "Jeannie, your father and I want to talk to you."

I didn't answer. All I wanted to do was rest. I wasn't sure my mind could deal with any more serious talking and my heart was already overloaded with conflicting feelings.

"Jeannie, did you hear me?" My mother was pleading.

I sensed how much she wanted to talk so I opened my eyes, sat up on the seat, took a deep breath and said, "Mom, I'm listening."

"You know your dad and I have been having some problems," Mom began. I glanced at Dad; he was intent on driving, but I knew he was listening. "Most of the problems have been because your dad and I just haven't been talking like we should. Just like we haven't been talking enough with you. We should have listened to you about Sam and we should have met Sam before we passed judgment on him."

"You'll like Sam, really you will."

"I hope we do, Jeannie, and we're going to make a real effort to listen to what you're saying to us from now on. And we're going to make an effort to listen to each other, too."

"Your mom's right, Jeannie. And Jeannie, I'm sorry about the things I said to you earlier this evening. I feel awful about what I said about your mother. I was so wrong." Dad looked at Mom in the most pleading way I'd ever seen him look. I felt terrible. I didn't want to be told all of this right now. I already had enough problems of my own. But I had to hear it.

"We know you have your own problems right now." How did she know what I was thinking? "So we don't want to burden you with ours. We wanted to protect you from all the bad in this world, but we know that's unrealistic. We tried to protect you too much. You're a very smart, mature young lady. You know far more about life than I did when I was fourteen."

"What your mom is trying to say is we're sorry about all the problems there have been at home. Your mother and I love each other very much and we're going to make sure things get better."

"That's right, and Jeannie, if there is anything at all we can do to make things easier for you, just tell us." Mom reached over the back of the seat and squeezed my hand. "Jeannie, we love you."

Those four simple words were my undoing. That and the warmth of my mother's hand brought tears streaming down my face. I sat in silence for the rest of the way as the tears washed my face.

When we got to Arly's, Sam's car was nowhere in sight. Instead, I saw Jeb's car and a police car. When

Dad parked, I went in. The same policemen who were at the house were talking to Jeb. I came close enough to hear Pearsly ask, "Was Jakness here when Sam was?"

"Yeah." Jeb nodded.

"Did they talk to each other?" O'Malley asked.

"Sort of."

"What does 'sort of' mean?"

"It wasn't exactly talking," Jeb answered.

"What exactly was it?" the policeman pressed.

"It was more like Jakness yelling at Sam and making lots of threats in between calling him names."

"What did Bensen do?"

"Not much," Jeb continued.

"Well, where are they now?" I was wondering the same thing.

"Around." Jeb looked at me and shrugged his shoulders. I couldn't stand it.

I stepped closer to Jeb and whispered to him, "I thought Sam was on his way to California."

"Not yet. I guess he just couldn't leave without seeing Jakness."

"But he promised," I said more to myself than Jeb.

"What are you two whispering about?" Pearsly asked.

"What's going on here? Where are those two?" O'Malley looked first at Jeb and then at me.

"I'm waiting. I feel trouble in the air and if you're really friends of Bensen you'll tell us where he is." Pearsly pointed at Jeb as he spoke.

"Jakness challenged him to a game of chicken and Sam accepted," Jeb finally answered.

"Oh, no." I could feel the blood racing to my head. The back of my throat tightened. I felt like I was going to vomit.

Immediately everyone was moving. "Where and when?" The cop was all business now.

"Any minute now," Jeb said softly, "and it's all that Jakness's fault." Jeb's voice rose as he talked.

"He wouldn't let Sam go. He kept threatening Sam and challenging him. He said he was going to kill him." By this time, Jeb was screaming; he was close to losing control. "I tried to stop them, JT, but I couldn't."

"Hey, kid, take it easy, we'll stop them." O'Malley put his hand on Jeb's shoulder.

"That man is crazy. He'll do anything to get Sam," Jeb said.

"Are they going to come down Fillmore?" Pearsly asked.

"Yeah," Jeb answered, "the usual way."

Mom and Dad were standing back of me. I must have looked sick. Mom stepped forward and put her hands on my shoulders. "Are you all right, Jeannie?"

"Yeah."

"You're shaking, honey."

"Jakness will kill him. Sam will never give in to him," I heard myself saying out loud.

"I know," Jeb answered.

"What are you all talking about?" Dad stepped up and spoke to Pearsly. O'Malley was speaking into his walkie-talkie.

"Chicken, Mr. Tanger," Pearsly began, "we're talking about chicken. It's one of the sickest games kids play around here. Two people get into their cars and drive in opposite directions. Then they turn around after they're a few blocks apart and drive straight at each other. The first driver to turn out is the chicken. Of course, if neither one turns out, nobody's a winner."

"Oh, my God, that's crazy." My dad was horrified. "I don't believe it!"

"You better believe it. From what I've heard about these two this game could get deadly." Pearsly voiced the screaming thoughts I was having.

O'Malley interrupted, "I've asked all the squads in the area to approach Fillmore immediately. Bensen has a green Volkswagen, doesn't he? And what's Jakness driving?"

"Yeah, Sam has a Volkswagen and Jakness is driving a red Corvette."

"Oh, great! Both cars will hold up like match sticks when they hit," O'Malley answered. He relayed the information over the walkie-talkie.

"Anybody know the turning-around points?" Pearsly looked at Jeb. He shook his head.

"You know what the rules are," Jeb said. The policeman nodded.

"What rules?" Dad asked.

"The drivers are the only ones who know the exact starting points and times. That way no one can tell the cops," I answered my father.

"This is crazy! Just block the streets," my father suggested.

"That's what we're trying to do, Mr. Tanger." O'Malley answered. "Unfortunately, there are too many places that they can start from: alleys, parking lots, side streets, you name it. Besides, Fillmore has a median, so we don't know which side they'll use either."

Just then we heard the screech of tires and all sound in the room stopped. The police were too late. The game had begun! O'Malley raced for the door. The rest of us were right behind him.

I could see the green bug coming down the street. It was at least a block away, but moving fast. In the opposite direction, I saw a red car zooming toward Sam. I knew it had to be Jakness.

All I could think of was Sam. How could he do this? Why did he have to be so stubborn? Maybe if I could just talk to him. Maybe then he would stop all this craziness. Suddenly I knew what I had to do and I felt my legs begin to move. I started running as fast as I could toward Sam's car. I had to stop him!

As I flew toward Sam, I realized the cars were

only about a block apart now. They were racing toward each other at breakneck speed. Somebody had to give soon. I could feel the snow on my face and the ground was snow-covered and slippery. I could hear someone screaming "Jeannie," but it had no connection with me. Someone was desperately trying to catch me. But I wasn't going to be caught.

I had crossed the south side of the street and was running down the median. By now the cars were only half a block apart and soon each would be committed to a course of action. The speed must have been sixty miles per hour.

"Sam, Sam, give it up!" My voice was carried away by the wind.

Both cars were still coming straight at each other. There was only one way to stop them. I jumped off the curb, ran into the middle of the street and began wildly waving my arms. I was facing Sam's car and it never crossed my mind that Jakness was driving right for me from behind.

Finally I could see Sam's face; he saw me at the same time. A look of recognition, confusion, and then horror crossed his face. He began frantically turning the wheel. I heard the screech of tires and saw the Volkswagen turning and heading over the curb. After that everything started to move in slow motion. When the front wheels hit the curb the back wheels started spinning on the ice. The back of the car slid sideways, hit the curb, and was lifted off the ground. Gusts of snow hit me in the face and that was the last I saw. I heard the crunch of metal and continuous popping and exploding sounds. I fell to my knees, trying to get away from the blasts of snow that were coming from every direction. All around me were screaming, crunching, slamming noises. Then everything was quiet. I felt someone lifting me up.

"Jeannie, Jeannie, are you all right?" It was Mom.

"He turned, did you see that? Sam turned. Everything is all right." Somehow I never connected the sound of breaking metal and smashed glass with Sam. All I could think of was that Sam veered and saved himself.

"Where's Sam?" I started to get up and then I saw it—or rather what was left of it. The green bug was upside down next to the smashed Corvette. Both cars were a mangled mass of torn and jagged metal. The wheels of the Volkswagen were spinning in the air and smoke was billowing with the snow, giving the appearance of thick fog. I saw Jeb and a policeman bending over Sam's car. I tried to move, but I felt strong hands gripping my shoulders, making me immobile.

"Jeannie, it's no use." My father's voice was behind the strong grip.

"Sam, I need to talk to Sam." I started pulling toward the car and my father reluctantly moved with me. As we approached the car, I heard the sirens in the background and I could see Jeb bent over Sam. Sam's body was trapped in the car. His eyes were open, but they were glassy. I knelt beside him and gently lifted his head with my hands.

"Hey, Just Terrific, what were you doing in the street?" His words were barely audible.

"Sam, I was afraid you wouldn't turn out. I know how stubborn you can be." I wasn't making any sense. Here Sam was lying in the snow, bleeding, and I was criticizing him.

"I turned out all right, but so did Jakness."

Then it dawned on me what had happened. "Sam, I, I..."

"JT, I love you," Sam whispered.

I felt my throat tighten and tears were on the verge of streaming down my face. "I love you too, Sam."

Sam's eyes closed and I felt his body relax. I hugged him tight.

Then men in white were moving me and bending

over Sam. I heard one of the medics say, "I can't find a pulse."

"No, no, he's all right!" I was screaming at them. They didn't know what they were talking about. My Sam was going to be all right.

"Get her out of here. She's in shock." I felt myself being pulled from Sam and then everything went blank.

Chapter 20

It's been nearly a year now. I finally went to the cemetery the other day. I was in the hospital during the funeral and for a long time after that. I couldn't really accept the fact that Sam had died. Now I can at least think about it, but I guess I probably will never totally accept it. For a long time, I blamed a lot of people for Sam's death. I thought adults were supposed to know everything. I didn't realize they get crazy, too. Like Jakness did. He lived and Sam died. I didn't think that was fair, but as Mom often tells me—life isn't fair, so don't expect it to be. Jakness did end up in a hospital somewhere, though, so maybe he wasn't so lucky after all. And my folks, I was mad at them, too. I didn't realize how unsure they were of things sometimes. I didn't know parents could make mistakes and still be O.K. Too bad I had to learn all of this in such a painful way. Sam's dad couldn't take it either. One day he just up and left. I think about him now and then and hope he's all right.

I'm back in school this year and things are better. I've had a lot of help from my best friend, Renee. She's been there through it all. I was sure wrong to think she didn't care about me. After all, best friends shouldn't be afraid to criticize or disagree about things. Just goes to show you how wrong I was about Renee. I'm even beginning to like Brian a little.

I'm doing all right at home, too. Mom and Dad are fine. Tom is away at college this year so Mom, Dad, and I spend a lot of time together. Lately, though, they've been getting on my nerves. Renee says that's healthy. Teenagers aren't supposed to get along too well with their parents, she says. I'm even dating a little. Jeb laughed at me the other day at lunch when I told him I had a date with a jock, but it was all in fun. We don't talk about Sam much, but when we do, I don't even cry. I guess that means I'm on my way up.

JEANETTE MINES RYAN grew up on a farm near Kimball, South Dakota. She graduated from the College of St. Teresa in Minnesota and received a Master's of Education from the University of Illinois. Currently she teaches English at Proviso West High School in Hillside, Illinois, and lives with her husband and daughter in Oak Park, Illinois.

NOVELS FROM AVON/FLARE

I LOVE YOU, STUPID!
Harry Mazer   61432-4/$2.5(
Marcus Rosenbloom is a high school senior whose mair
problem in life is being a virgin. His dynamic relation
ship with the engaging Wendy Barrett, and his contin
uing efforts to "become a man," show him that neithe
sex, nor friendship—nor love—is ever very simple.

CLASS PICTURES
Marilyn Sachs   61408-1/$1.9!
When shy, plump Lolly Scheiner arrives in kindergar
ten, she is the "new girl everyone hates," and only popu
lar Pat Maddox jumps to her defense. From then or
they're best friends through thick and thin, supporting
each other during crises until everything changes in
eighth grade, when Lolly suddenly turns into a thin
pretty blonde and Pat, an introspective science whiz
finds herself playing second fiddle for the first time.

JACOB HAVE I LOVED
Katherine Paterson   56499-8/$1.9!
Do you ever feel that no one understands you? Louise'
pretty and talented twin sister, Caroline, has always
been the favored one, while Louise is ignored and mis
understood. Now Louise feels that Caroline has stolen
from her all that she has ever wanted...until she learns
how to fight for the love, and the life she wants for her
self. "Bloodstirring." *Booklist* A Newbery Award
winner.

NOVELS FROM AVON/FLARE

THE GROUNDING OF GROUP 6
by Julian Thompson

Coming in May 1983!
83386-7/$2.50

What do parents do when they realize that their six-teen-year old son or daughter is a loser and an embarassment to the family? If they are wealthy and have contacts, they can enroll their kids in Group 6 of the exclusive Coldbrook Country School, and the eccentric, diabolical Dr. Simms will make sure that they become permanently "grounded"—that is, murdered. When the five victims discover they are destined to "disappear"—and that their parents are behind the evil plot—they enlist the help of Nat, their group leader, to escape.

AFTER THE FIRST DEATH
by Robert Cormier

62885-6/$2.50

This shattering thriller is about a group of terrorists who hijack a school bus in New England and hold a group of children hostage—forcing each one to make decisions that will affect not only their own lives, but also the nation. "Marvelously told...The pressure mounts steadily." *The New York Times* "Haunting...Chilling ..Tremendous." *Boston Globe*

TAKING TERRI MUELLER
by award-winning Norma Fox Mazer

79004-1/$2.25

Was it possible to be kidnapped by your own father? For as long as Terri could remember, she and her father had been a family—alone together. Her mother had died nine years ago in a car crash—so she'd been told. But now Terri has reason to suspect differently, and as she struggles to find the truth on her own, she is torn between the two people she loves most.

Available wherever paperbacks are sold or directly from the publisher. Include 50¢ per copy for postage and handling; allow 6-8 weeks for delivery. Avon Books, Mail Order Dept., 224 W. 57th St., N.Y., N.Y. 10019

Flare Bstsllrs 3-83B

Flare Novels
For Young Adults

AN X-RATED ROMANCE   79905-7/$1.95
by Tina Sunshine
In this wildly funny tale of infatuation, Sara and Emily
are best friends—and partners in crime. Because of a
lack of O.B.s—Older Boys—in their school, Sara has a
hopeless crush on their eighth grade teacher, Mr. Garfield, and the two girls come up with several uproar-
ious schemes to get Mr. Garfield to notice Sara.

END OF SUMMER   79293-1/$2.25
by Bernice Grohskopf
Sixteen year-old Maggie spends July as a mother's
helper in Maine, while her best friend, Jan, works at
home. In Maine, Maggie falls in love with a dashing,
young Englishman, Tony Wilson, and when Maggie
has to go back home, Tony insists on visiting her.
There, Tony and Jan become attracted to one
another. Feeling betrayed, Maggie is crushed and
angry, but learns some valuable lessons.

AVON Paperback

FLARE NOVELS
FROM BESTSELLING AUTHOR
NORMA KLEIN

BREAKING UP   59972-4/$2.25

When 15-year-old Ali Rose goes to visit her father and his new wife in California, she expects a carefree summer. But Ali's summer turns out to be a time of impossible decisions. She is forced to make a choice in the custody battle between her divorced parents and between her possessive best friend and a new love.

IT'S NOT WHAT   59253-3/$1.95
YOU'D EXPECT

Carla and Oliver, 14-year-old twins, are angry and confused about their father's decision to go to New York to work on his novel—and leave the family behind. But as the summer progresses, Carla and Oliver are presented with more perplexing problems. Together they come to understand their parent's unsteady marriage—and their own young adulthood.

MOM, THE WOLFMAN   59998-8/$1.95
AND ME

Brett—sensible and thoroughly modern—loves the unconventional life she leads. But when her unmarried mom meets an attractive, unattached man with an Irish wolfhound, Brett begins to worry that she may do something crazy—like get married! This novel, which was made into a television movie was called "a remarkable book" by *The New York Times*.

TAKING SIDES 60004-8/$1.95

When their parents are divorced, Nell and her five-year-old brother, Hugo go to live with their father. There are many adjustments to be made and Nell sometimes wishes for a more normal life. But she gradually grows to accept her lifestyle, and, finally she discovers it is possible to love both her parents at the same time.

SUNSHINE 80341-0/$2.25

Jacquelyn Helton died at the age of 20 from a rare form of bone cancer. Her story tells what it's like to die, to leave a husband and two-year-old daughter behind and to try to squeeze every ounce of love and happiness into a sadly short period of time. An acclaimed CBS television movie, SUNSHINE "bursts with the joy and fulfillment of living."

Los Angeles Times